Waist Deep

Waist Deep

LINEA MAJA ERNST

Translated from the Danish by
Sherilyn Nicolette Hellberg

JONATHAN CAPE
LONDON

1 3 5 7 9 10 8 6 4 2

UK | USA | Canada | Ireland | Australia
India | New Zealand | South Africa

Jonathan Cape, an imprint of Vintage, is part of the Penguin
Random House group of companies whose addresses can
be found at global.penguinrandomhouse.com

Vintage, Penguin Random House UK,
One Embassy Gardens, 8 Viaduct Gardens, London SW11 7BW

penguin.co.uk/vintage
global.penguinrandomhouse.com

First published by Jonathan Cape in 2025

Set in 12.4 pt/17 pt Calluna
Typeset by Jouve (UK), Milton Keynes

Printed and bound in Great Britain by Clays Ltd, Elcograf S.p.A.

The authorised representative in the EEA is Penguin Random House
Ireland, Morrison Chambers, 32 Nassau Street, Dublin D02 YH68

A CIP catalogue record for this book is available from the British Library

ISBN 9781787335646

Penguin Random House is committed to a sustainable future
for our business, our readers and our planet. This book is made
from Forest Stewardship Council® certified paper.

Cast of Characters

Sylvia Pathological daydreamer. Dating Charlie
    and confused.

Quince Charmer. A bachelor in a sea of couples.

Gry Goddess of care. Married to Adam, mother
    to Vera and Sejr.

Esben Writer, mild-mannered and a little
    reserved. Engaged to Karen.

Karen Tall, commanding, objectively beautiful.
    A born queen.

Charlie Absolute dreamboat of a girlfriend.
    Looks like a fairy-tale prince.

Adam Bureaucrat, clean-cut. Father to Vera and
    Sejr. Not un-princely either.

Vera and Sejr The kids.

Day 1

Sylvia tries to get comfortable in the backseat. She reclines, shifts around, puts her feet up on the driver's seat. She loves how transparent Charlie's ears are, her backlit skin conch red. Sylvia tickles her earlobe with her big toe.

Charlie gives Sylvia's foot a squeeze.

'Could you sit up, please?'

Sylvia thinks that the rules of traffic shouldn't apply to the forest, but she straightens up anyway, sits cross-legged instead. She notices her knickers are bunched, so she unbuttons her shorts, sticks her hand down into them, runs a finger along her labia, sliding between them, and adjusts the cotton fabric. She cups her hand beneath her nose; she's always loved the smell: briny, whitish, floral.

Sylvia read somewhere that if you dab a bit behind your ears like perfume, it'll work like an aphrodisiac.

She dabs behind her ears, runs her fingers through her hair.

Through the window, the woods slide past. The tarmac road turns to gravel, the summer light dims. They drive through the older part of the woods.

1

Midsummer is approaching and everything is green and plump with moisture. The beech trees are knotty, the moss aglow and luminescent. There are large wind-fallen trees with their roots in the air; there are pines, seven-trunked beech clusters twisting their crowns up and over the woodland road, their reflections glistening on the bumper of the old dark-purple Volvo, a square retiree that Charlie has sentimentally insisted on keeping; she fixes it up herself.

'Don't you want to learn how to drive?' Charlie asks her now and then; and Sylvia says she's too scattered, always spacing out, prone to panicking, hands aflutter, and when you've just run someone over at a crossing, that kind of behaviour isn't cute anymore.

Charlie is a calm driver, her hands resting on the wheel. Sylvia can't take her eyes off them. She can't help but see it as coded, the driving licence, as butch, as grown up, a sign of having your act together. Of course, in the countryside, here in Himmerland, everyone has a driving licence. But metropolitan kids age differently.

And see practical necessities like a driving licence as intriguing forms of personal expression.

Sylvia considers herself a backseat type, a passenger princess. She likes to be driven, she loves it when Charlie picks her up.

Charlie, who feels like home, like a boulder in the sun. Their eyes meet in the rear-view mirror; Charlie's moss-green eyes. She smiles.

'Are you tired?'

'No, I'm excited! We haven't seen each other in ages.'

'Remind me. What kind of house is it again?'

'A forester's lodge,' Sylvia explains. 'Karen's parents own it.'

Charlie suppresses a grin.

'And what exactly is a forester's lodge?'

'Actually . . . I don't know.'

Charlie laughs.

'But it sounds very romantic and particular, which I love!'

'Of course, your friends don't just have a normal Danish summerhouse,' Charlie smiles as she signals to turn, following the rules, even though the gravel road is deserted. 'They are also very romantic and particular and articulate.'

'They're nice!' Sylvia says.

'Yes, they're nice.'

Charlie ought to, Sylvia thinks, be able to romanticise living conditions. Her houseboat, where they live most of the time, is beyond dreamy. How the bed is a nest at the stern, how the whole boat rocks with the weather and their movements (sublime sex on a thundery night). There are little niches in all the surfaces to hold things, hooks for the mugs. Those antediluvian windows; are they called portholes?

Sylvia loves the boat, Charlie helping her on deck, catching her, wrapping an arm around her waist.

But she's tired of the eternal maintenance, the practical tasks; something perpetually in need of repair. At least, Charlie looks fantastic scraping barnacles off the keel when she takes the boat out of the water. Charlie is good with her hands, whereas Sylvia's university friends are garrulous, gushing; it makes her insecure.

'I've got you,' Sylvia says.

Esben and Karen have already arrived. The house is right by the lake, and the map on Charlie's phone starts glitching; the service is bad, the roads in the woods are ancient.

Gry is on her way too, somewhere nearby.

'Have you always been so close? Even at university?' Charlie asks.

'At first, mostly just Esben and me and Karen were friends. And then Quince and I bonded. And Karen and Gry have become really close over the past few years – they're both in similar places with their adult jobs and serious relationships.'

Charlie looks at her in the mirror.

'But yeah, we're all really close,' Sylvia smiles.

They've been driving for hours; they left Copenhagen around noon, and it's almost evening now, but there's still light in the sky. Gry had made a plan for them all weeks ago, taking the coordination upon herself: 'Why don't we aim to get there by dinnertime? That would work best for the kids.'

Sylvia wishes the kids could have stayed at home with their dinner times and bedtimes, but she can't wait to throw her arms around her friends. To see Esben. She likes the person she becomes when he's there.

Charlie clears her throat.

'I can see the lake ahead. Should we wake up Quince?'

Quince has been sleeping next to Sylvia for most of the journey, his head resting on the window; he had apologised when they picked him up, hungover from the previous night, a trace of blue-green glitter on his cheekbone. It shimmers in the evening sun. Quince had been out dancing, ended up jumping in the harbour at dawn with some new friends; it had all started with a poetry reading. If it had been up to him, they wouldn't have left until the afternoon, but he made a valiant effort, chatting with Charlie and Sylvia for the first leg of the drive, and now he's been sleeping since Funen. Between stifled yawns, Quince told them about his night, about meeting Cosmos, the most beautiful man he'd ever seen, though regretfully they only shook hands. Then he conked out. Sylvia admires that about Quince, how easily he falls for people and how easily he lets them go.

They turn down an even smaller road, bony with crisscrossing roots, soft with pine needles, which leads them across the little peninsula that juts out into the lake. Here, you're hidden. Bluish pines. A strip of shore; clear water over the glittering lakebed. A fire pit.

They park by the edge of the water. Sylvia turns to Quince, tickles his knee to wake him up. He draws up his shoulders, shivers awake.

And there's the house, just as the forest becomes a

forest. Black-painted logs between the birch trees, stone foundation, a thick golden thatched roof and a terrace catching the sunshine. It looks like it's been here for ages, robust; the chimney suggests a fireplace. At the same time, the white gazebo-like frames hugging the swollen windowpanes make it seem refined. Climbing roses clamber over the windbreak, and there is Esben. He waves enthusiastically, walks over to meet them with out-stretched arms, an awkwardness to his body language, both effusive and stiff, as if he's overcoming his innate shyness, insisting on being warm-hearted. It's irresistible. Sylvia is already out of the car, falling into Esben's arms. His stubble, his shirt, the thin fabric of his shorts. He shaved his head recently, and it's already growing back: dark against the thin frames of his glasses. He looks like a German idealist poet, distant and romantic, like a tarot-card page, a boyish feudal prince.

But here he is, in the flesh. She feels him relax against her, swaying slightly; he folds his arms around her. This is no cordial hug; he squeezes her tight, and she takes a deep breath, her nose pressed against the collar of his shirt.

'It's so good to see you!'

Sylvia carefully frees herself so Esben can greet Charlie and Quince.

*

Quince awakes to a buzzing landscape, to Sylvia, Charlie and Esben talking. He blinks the sleep away, succumbing to the view. The twilight sky is watercolour red, the forest burning with fireweed and poppies. The grass looks soft, inviting. Madum Lake is quiet and dazzling; the silver birch trees stand watch, dipping their catkins into the water, their leaves quivering on bowed branches; a curtain wanting to be drawn, a hushed drumroll.

He feels the anticipation bubbling up. How enchanting! A week in the woods, by the lake, all of them together again. We can celebrate and sunbathe and make lavish dinners, sit outside in the summer night, deep in conversation until the sun rises. It'll be like our own clever talk show, fabulous and never-ending. Maybe we'll go skinny dipping? Throw a rave in the woods? His suitcase is full of fantastic outfits.

For years, they've been admonishing each other, saying that they need to get together more often. But time passes, three months, then six. Another baby, more obligations. A new job, mortgages. They're all becoming more set in their ways. But they're also more mature, less insecure.

Back when they were students, Quince wasn't really there. Not wholeheartedly. Part of him always felt like he wasn't able to be himself. But now he's finally living out his youth, or maybe something better. He wants to share it with the rest of them.

He looks out at the lake, feeling the others' gazes tethered to his.

The water is smooth and purple. A spray of white

aquatic plants skirts the shore. It makes you want to hop right in. Quince shuts his eyes.

Takes it all in: This place romanticises itself.

Karen throws open the terrace doors, steps into the evening sun to receive her friends. She waves but stays where she is. They go to her. Karen has always been a vision. Long elvish hair, her swan's neck, divine cheekbones; she's only got slimmer with age, but stronger too; there's a strength to her that doesn't require muscle, that stands out all the more in her fragility. She looks like a princess, but she is a knight, a fortress.

Quince has the urge to kneel, not in a romantic way, but as a courtly ritual, to call on her beauty, her dignity, the warm light of the evening sun finding her like a projector, but she would think he was making fun of her; she's not theatrically inclined. Instead, he hugs her, they all do, one by one; the hug is their preferred greeting, equalising, amorphous, their bodies melting platonically together. Karen tolerates it, she doesn't really like hugs. Quince wonders with a smile whether she would have preferred him to kneel before her after all, alas!

He wouldn't call Karen nice per se, but she's just – there's something unyielding about her, something good and steely. Quince remembers when they all went to Bakken for his twenty-fifth birthday and he was so touched, by how they understood him, how they indulged his childish impulses, the joy of cheering, shrieking on the rides, the candyfloss. They'd been waiting in line, Karen and him, the only ones brave enough to try the most daunting rollercoaster. She probably wasn't that into the idea, but she didn't want him to have to go alone. He was overjoyed, pulling her to the end of the platform, to the last car, as he explained that it was most fun to sit at the very back, where the drop was biggest, the rush in your belly greatest – and as Karen was nodding, listening intently, a few teenage boys snuck past. Quince was willing to let it go. They're just kids, he told himself, and something about groups of teenage boys always made him nervous. 'Hey!' Karen shouted. 'We're waiting for that car – you can't just jump the queue.' He loved her for that: scolding the kids, her sense of principle, that he was under her protection.

Karen shows them to their rooms. Quince gets the west-facing room, with a view of the lake and the sunset. This is a bachelor's room; light wood walls, a single bed, a washstand at the window in oak with a bright marble top, a shaving bowl, a white enamel washing jug, a bouquet of wildflowers already sprinkling the marble slab, an old mirror with green-speckled glass. Karen waits in the doorway.

'I hope you like it. My parents decorated the place. It's a little too much.'

'I love when things are too much,' Quince beams. 'A gable room!'

'No, a gable room would be upstairs or under the eaves,' Karen corrects him, before turning to show Sylvia and Charlie their room. Quince bites his tongue. He opens the window to the hollyhocks gently knocking against the frame, shepherding in the evening air, the scent of elderflowers hanging in the air like sweet dust, mixing with the smell of fresh water. He almost can't handle it: the view, the potential; it reminds him of a film, but which one; the lazy summer night, the sun, tall white flowers in overgrown grass; he doesn't know what they're called, but they scream *June!* He almost wishes he were more buttoned-up, reserved, so he could let go, whipped up by the sun-ripe days and the forest, loosen a tie, but he's already as loose as can be; he doesn't even know how to knot a tie, but one of the others could probably show him. He's good at asking for help.

The landscape also reminds him of *Thunderclump*, the children's film that takes place over one long Scandinavian summer night when the toys come to life. He was a daydreamer as a child; he still is, and how can you not be when the trees are huddled up like a dark, midsummer green choir? It recalls something Greek, something Shakespearean. He imagines a Puck, a Pan, a sexy faun, in the woods, in the reeds. Nimble, half-naked. With a crown of morning glory, maybe wearing clothes left by lovers on the forest floor: stockings like long, smoke-coloured gloves, a ripped-open shirt, lacy pants. Tousled hair and clear eyes. If this were a film or a play, Puck would step out to introduce the plot, hands gleefully rubbing together: six friends – one week – a summerhouse.

But then he hears a distant growl. Another car arrives, masterfully parks. A snow-grey Tesla, the ultimate family vehicle, its brutal sensibility puncturing the pastoral scene. Quince watches from the window. It was all too arcadian anyway, he thinks. A little contrast is good, and now Gry is here, thank God; he hates waiting.

Gry alights, a squall of curls kept in place by French plaits, puff sleeves, exquisite hips in expensive mum jeans. Quince loves her brawny driving, that she can make a Tesla rumble. She's otherwise so mild-mannered. Now she's unpacking her buttermilk-blond kids from the backseat. Vera and Sejr are sticky and swollen from the heat, but maybe that's just how kids look. Vera must be five by now, Sejr around three.

The other door opens.

Oh no. Is he here too?

He steps out of the car. Tall and blond. A sun god with a political science degree. There are some men who look like sculptures of Apollo, whose features are so regular that they almost appear rational; clean-cut vitalism boys, the worst. You can see in Adam that he's been the picture of health since he was a child, athletic with spiky blond hair. The boy you both feared and secretly admired in the playground. A particular expression of masculinity: cultured rather than coarse, comfortable in his skin and thus even more intimidating. Oxford shirt. Fresh trim.

Quince turns from the window.

Gry usually comes by herself with a good excuse for Adam. Quince has only met him a handful of times. Officially, because he's working, as an adviser or director, or whatever he is, at one of the ministries. Quince can't remember which, only that it is an important one (that requires responsibility, calm brutality behind a standing desk, presumably), but he assumes the excuses have more to do with Adam's distaste for their group of literary, eccentric artist types, over-the-top queers. Well, he's not going to let Adam ruin his idyllic vision for the week, even if he's walking around looking like a *Euroman* ad.

He revises the cast: six friends and Adam.

Quince falls backwards onto the single bed. He catches a glimpse of himself in the mirror among the pillowcases, golden-red in the rays from the low sun; he shakes out his curls; swooning suits him. He considers for a moment: Do you say swoon, or faint? There used to be more words to describe flinging yourself down dramatically. He would like to reinstate them.

Esben knocks on the door. Quince props himself up on an elbow.

'Gry and Adam are here. Are you ready for dinner?'

*

Adam offers his hand, introduces himself.

'We've met before,' Quince says.

'Oh right . . . what's your name again, Pomegranate?'

'Quince,' says Quince, narrowing his eyes. They take

their seats out on the terrace. Karen stands up at the head of the table, ready to introduce the meal Esben has prepared.

'Let's eat! On the menu tonight we have grilled perch from the lake, which Esben caught, *illegally*.'

They laugh at Karen's scandalised tone. Esben smiles, looking down at the table, seeming both apologetic and a little proud. Sheepishly, he adds:

'But there are so many of them out there, waiting to be caught!'

'And what else are we having?'

A cassava mash, a traditional South American dish, whipped stiff with starch. Esben placidly explains that the root contains cyanide, that if you don't peel and prepare it properly, it can kill you. Normally, this type of information would make Sylvia panic, and the casual threat of collective cyanide poisoning does make her anxious, but with Esben, she would rather run the risk and appear cosmopolitan and easy-going in his eyes. She strokes the antique silverware. And in the worst case, at least they would die together.

It's been twelve years since they first met: Sylvia, Esben, Karen, Gry and Quince, who was called something else back then. They biked through the early morning haze, filed into the lecture theatre. They were thinner, trepidatious. Their eyes were on the blackboard, on each other. Literary theory, cultural theory, semester after semester. They idolised their professors, who were Olympic gods, magnificent and fallible, each one a type: a Lacanian genius, an awkward Marxist in Balenciaga, a middle-aged professor known for leaning in too close to his female students, an elegant lock of hair falling over his forehead. He flirts with everyone, Sylvia had sulked at the time, offended; why doesn't he want to flirt with me?

They gossiped about their professors, bonding between lectures, flopped onto threadbare couches in the student bar, ordering the cheapest coffee and beer they would ever drink. Eventually, they admitted how little of the theory they understood, but they got smarter, sharper, in the soporific library light; they developed their own personal tastes, an interest in ecocriticism, gender studies, the Bloomsbury Group, New Journalism. Bent over their books they thought to themselves: I'm a failure, and then: Everyone in this library wants me.

Each of them had been the brightest in their secondary-school class, and while they were relieved to have finally found a home, they also had to suffer the unforeseen humiliation of being average, mediocre, for the first time in their lives. They didn't know who they were anymore. They were more themselves than ever. They were longing to be seen, but couldn't bear to be known. They threw parties in the tiny student accommodation they shared with three other room-mates. They drank ironic piña coladas from unironic mason jars. They became friends, fell in love with each other. If two of them kissed one night, it didn't mean anything, but if they slept together, maybe that meant something? Karen and Esben started sleeping together with the simultaneous ease and self-consciousness with which they approached everything back then. Sylvia had thought, this is a phase, like everything else. But instead, Esben and Karen got more and more serious, travelled the world together, returned home; and they've been together ever since.

They have all settled into serious relationships, serious lives.

They used to see each other every day, now they see each other rarely. They haven't lost touch intentionally, it's just what happens. They've had kids, coupled off, started careers; they have things to take care of now. They see each other at the playground; they meet for coffee; they hear about each other's lives, but they aren't part of them.

It's been too long, but now they're finally together again. Sylvia takes in her friends around the table. Now they are here, now the sun is setting and the blackbirds are singing and there's blackcurrant wine and the birch trees are swooshing, and if anyone breathes a word about interest rates, she'll start screaming and never stop.

Esben, their bashful poet turned poacher. He's wearing the same worn, raspberry-red suede jacket he's had since they were students.

Gry leans toward him.

'I just finished your book, Esben. It was so touching. I'm going to give it to everyone I know,' she says.

'Oh, thank you. I'm so happy to hear that.' He smiles but seems not to want to say more about it. Esben is polite, uncomfortable in the spotlight. The past few months must have been hard on him, Sylvia thinks. His first two books were small, serious, formally experimental, hits for a niche crowd. The first, a collection of understated poetry, and then a literary meditation on the lives of saints. But his new one, a novel about his mother, was an instant sensation.

Esben passes Adam a platter: bitter endive, rosehip leaves, redcurrants gleam against the expensive beige fabric of his Oxford shirt. Adam is presenting the wines he and Gry brought: 'This one is pure and simple, no nonsense, desiccated grapes from a dry season, relentless sunshine, pure taste, a very winy wine. This one has a rougher mouthfeel, dirty and barnyardy.'

Gry is happy that Adam came. Karen had told her beforehand about her ulterior motive, the secret plan for the holiday, why it was crucial they were all there. Gry enjoyed being in the know. Her friends don't really know Adam, but they would like him if they got to know him, and he can always talk to Karen. She and Adam are made of the same stuff. They have always seen the latest episode of *Debatten*, and are ready to discuss what was or wasn't said at this or that press conference. Adam isn't tight-lipped about his work. He is unsparingly honest. He makes his own rules. Right now, for example, he's talking to Karen about the minister he technically works for but doesn't respect.

Karen listens while Adam speaks, but she won't let herself be charmed by his confidence. She crosses her arms, asks him pointed questions. Adam talks faster, as he does when he is trying to convince somebody that he is right. Karen is someone you want to measure up to. Gry is used to turning the small pangs of envy into affection; otherwise, you can't be in her company. You have to be content in her orbit. Karen has probably never second-guessed her beauty or her intelligence, Gry thinks. How is it even possible to be a woman without an inferiority complex, without imposter syndrome? Karen is unstoppable; she enters meeting rooms with the poise of Margaret Thatcher and the face of Grace Kelly. Karen used to work as a model back when they were students, but she never spoke about modelling as if it were trivial, or beneath her. She consistently introduced herself as the journalist she became and let her modelling career expire as soon as she was hired full time. Now, she's an editor at a major newspaper, domestic affairs. She and Esben, the ultimate power couple.

Esben gets up to go inside. He pauses behind Sylvia's chair and musses her hair, the dark bird's nest that is always coming apart, falling over her shoulders. She's wearing a thin camisole, no bra. Gry wants to hear what Sylvia has been up to; there's always a new project. Sylvia has a different, fluttering confidence; she's always seemed so free, at home in her anti-career. She works as a guide at a deserted museum; she is always writing things that never seem to go anywhere: a television script, a book of essays. At some point, she started painting, then she spent two months in Canada working on a regenerative farm. Mercurial, manic Sylvia. She looks up happily, the sun on her face, and puts her hand on Esben's.

'Wow, everything is so delicious! And it's so beautiful here! I'm so happy that we're all here together!'

The children let themselves be put to bed. Gry is back at the table in under fifteen minutes. She feels the old atmosphere buzzing around them, around the whole table. Finally, they are back together again. The conversation runs down familiar paths, old jokes, stupid but carefully chosen darlings. Should they put on some music? Some B-list flops? Maybe the crown prince's fiftieth-birthday playlist? Do we say the King now? What about David Owe's album? Or the Michael Carøe one with the English covers, Gry chimes in, and the others agree. She's relieved to get it right.

The night is generous; the light hangs around, as if boasting: *Oh my, is it nine o'clock already? Well, I suppose I could stay another hour.* Dusk arrives, slow and pastel blue, its arm draped around the sunset like an embrace. Maybe just one more glass?

'What do we need to do?' Gry asks. 'Should we make a plan for the week? We can take turns cooking.' She offers to make a chart.

Is she about to start clearing the table? Quince wonders, sinking lower into his chair, hanging on the armrest, but not because Gry seems frazzled. It's easy to relax in her presence; she doesn't make you feel bad about it; she's so caring in her essence. Lots of people become worn out, sunken, depleted from becoming mothers, but Gry's maternalism is natural, sublime. She has always been so strong and feminine. Back when they were students, she wore a yoga mat slung over her shoulder every day like a quiver, and she still looks girlish with that shock of hair, her elaborate plaits and rosy cheeks. And yet she seems to be an eternal mother, carrying her children with those fantastic arms, bluish veins twisting and spreading down to the backs of her hands. She could be in a garden with a jug on her hip, a checked handkerchief around her head: she has phenomenal posture. And now she's taking out her knitting, her calm aura enveloping them all. As if at any moment a deer might pad over and rest its head in her lap. He wants to rest his head in her lap. To fall and hurt himself so she can comfort him. Maybe the reason motherhood suits Gry so well is because she has always been a mother to them, Quince thinks. But she's not homely. Her knitting, her rhubarb preserves couldn't be more modern. Right now, she's knitting a green and brown vest top that looks like something from the National Museum, a hipster bog-girl outfit, and there are rose peppercorns in the jars of jam she brought along because she couldn't help herself.

Quince refills Gry's glass with deep red blackcurrant

vermouth, a little Campari, a splash of gin, precariously close to the rim, as if to keep her in her seat.

'Now, don't you try to take care of anything. The only thing you need to worry about is getting a little drunk,' he says.

Just try to be nonchalant, Gry tells herself, *relax*, but it's difficult, she can get so overwhelmed by how brilliant her friends are, how interesting, the ease with which they express themselves; they've only become more radiant, more eccentric, more themselves with time. Just look at Quince, lining his glass up next to hers, pouring himself a tall summer Negroni.

On Quince's other side, Sylvia is resting her head on his shoulder, her best, pleasure-loving friend, tipsy in the evening sun. Could Sylvia love anyone more? Quince, who seems younger than the rest of them, maybe because he's just gone through his second puberty. Quince, all gentle cleverness. He teaches film and media at a secondary school, and his students are probably all in love with him, willing to endure Pasolini marathons for him. Soft, bleached curls, the reddish hue of a box dye's cheap chemistry, bronze eyes, a tawny tan. He looks like someone Zeus might kidnap, who would resist, but mostly for the drama of it. Ganymede in a crop top or white vest or now, better, finally, bare-chested. Borne by the tender vanity on his new body's behalf, the meticulously built muscle; he has been careful not to pump too hard.

'Anyone want a beer?' Adam asks. He's already on his feet, bringing a few bottles back to the table.

(Of course he needs a beer right now, Quince thinks, but it isn't just about the beer – it's an excuse to do something, practical type that he is, always needing to be productive.)

Adam sits down next to Charlie, who hasn't touched her glass of wine. She takes a beer, passes her cigarettes to Adam; a silent, amicable transaction. Charlie, Quince thinks tenderly, who is so androgynous, like a medieval angel, muscular and soft. Quince nudges Sylvia, so she can appreciate Charlie's beauty too, and Sylvia follows his gaze, sees the ray of light landing on Charlie exhaling smoke against the sunset. Quince and Sylvia let out a collective sigh: smoking suits Charlie so well, and the table too as the smoke catches the light. Sylvia is grateful that she and Quince can share this moment of adoration. They're both equally gushy, have always worked each other up about people or things or the last rays of sunlight colliding in a jug of water, crashing in copper waves across the table, into Charlie's tousled hair, golden on golden. Someone has to notice, after all, and they always do.

Sylvia points to the lake, to the bluish gleam suspended over the shallows and the tall stems topped with fine, light-blue flowers growing out of the water.

'Does anybody know what those plants by the lake are called?'

Gry lights up. This is *all* her.

'Those are lobelias! Actually, the lake is called a *lobelia lake*, because of the flowers. They only grow in a few places in Jutland, where the water is clear enough for the light to reach the bottom. In folklore, people use lobelia as love amulets. You're supposed to pick the flowers in midsummer.'

This is what Gry is working on at the university – *hydromythology*, a project at the crossroads of eco-criticism and folk studies. Wetlands as a topos of endangered botany and Scandinavian folklore. She studies sources related to traditional medicine, local myths about sea creatures and the coast, variations on the Nixie, the river man. On the drive, she told the children about the Brook Horse, a fearsome, magical creature who lures his victims into the depths of lakes and tributaries. Yes, from *Frozen II*, Vera said with a knowing nod. This lake is supposed to be enchanted; Gry reminds herself to ask Karen about it, the wicked spirits.

'Lobelias are hermaphroditic and reproduce asexually,' Gry adds. 'They're kind of queer, you could even say.' Sylvia smiles politely, makes an effort not to roll her eyes; instead, she kicks Quince's foot under the table and receives a smug bump in response. Sylvia and Quince have talked about this before, about how only heterosexual academics would ever think to call a plant queer because to them everything that's slightly odd, slightly off-kilter, is totally gay and exciting.

Now the twilight means business, turning into dusk, and reluctantly they agree to break up the party while they can still see. Gry starts to clear the table.

*

Charlie and Sylvia settle in, or rather Sylvia lounges on the bed while Charlie rummages through their bags. She throws a tote bag to Sylvia, a surprise. Inside: a bag of Sylvia's favourite sweets, cheap milk chocolate she would *never* eat in front of the others, and a pair of wide brown leather handcuffs, supple from use. Charlie looks up.

'Are you in the mood for this or that, or both? Your choice, honey.'

Sylvia beams. Sometimes she forgets how spoiled, how lucky, she is. Charlie takes such good care of her. She lies back, shuts her eyes, feels the alcohol and the evening sun through the window warming her cheeks. Charlie crawls over to her, pushes a knee between her legs, separates them.

Charlie grabs Sylvia's hips, flips her over, pulls her up onto her knees. Sylvia arches her back; she's wet, heavy, just from the way Charlie treats her; she's so strong, so caring, so safe. And yet: a predatory instinct.

'What do you want, baby?'

Something changes, turns insistent, hungry, in Charlie's voice as she deftly ties Sylvia's hands around her back, snaps the leather cuffs around her wrists, runs her fingers through Sylvia's hair.

'I want you to be rough with me.'

Sylvia's voice is already broken. Charlie presses her face into the pillow and Sylvia writhes, plays resistant, whines, but only to make Charlie tighten her grasp. Charlie slaps her two times, hard, quick. Sylvia feels the blood filling the imprint of a palm on one of her buttocks. Charlie puts her hand to the mark, feels Sylvia submit, whimpering.

'Don't move.'

Sylvia loves the determination, the difference in Charlie's voice, the feeling of the pillowcase against her cheek, how flushed she gets, the heat, the cool fabric, her skin goosebumped and burning; the redness in her face, her arse, her cunt, getting wet, swelling, getting tight, soft, around Charlie's two fingers pushing into her. It's too much, too fast. She moans, 'You're too big, Daddy.'

The dirty talk started as a joke, but then it actually worked, so it became part of their repertoire. Charlie shushes her, whispers in her ear; her fingers moving faster, rhythmically.

'Be quiet – everyone can hear you.'

She's teasing her, Sylvia knows. Charlie isn't embarrassed, she loves Sylvia's sounds. In company, Charlie is more reserved, tries not to draw attention to herself or say the wrong thing. Among Sylvia's friends, she is the only one who didn't study the humanities or social sciences, who doesn't worship subtle irony.

Sylvia moans, shuts her eyes. She likes that it hurts,

and even though Charlie doesn't know what she's punishing her for, it feels good. She looks over her shoulder, at Charlie's wheaten hair, her sweaty forehead, tireless forearms. When they're in bed together, Charlie is a god; she's psychic, she's inside Sylvia's head, she knows how to move, how to make Sylvia's body vibrate; she feels Sylvia glowing inside, blows on the embers.

Sylvia lets go of her thoughts, lets Charlie hold them instead; she flows into her body, the swells; she holds her breath, tenses her abdominal muscles; it's hard to come like this, on her stomach, on her knees, but the orgasms are better, she can feel years of accumulated tension easing, her muscles and complexes melting away, a thaw, rushing through her, surging from her belly up through her spine, spilling into her brain, out of her mouth.

And Sylvia doesn't care if anyone hears them, that she can't keep her voice in her throat when she comes, into the pillow – a broken sound of gratitude, something between a moan and a melody; she is full and trembling; there isn't anywhere she'd rather be.

Day 2

It's early morning. Now they've settled, now they're ready to get going. Adam found a cast-iron pot in the toolshed last night, and a cooking stand with a chain to hang the pot over a fire. A project. As soon as he woke up, he went outside to get to work, smoke mingling with the fog over the lake in the rosy morning. He grabs the olive oil, a can of tomatoes and a bowl of vegetables, and sits at the table – in running shorts, a wool sweater – slicing onions, garlic, peppers, aubergines, the beginnings of a shakshuka, a dark-red stew. He imagines a cool morning in the mountains – which mountains though; are they in the Middle East or Northern Africa, does it even matter? This pot is incredible. When everyone else wakes up, his shakshuka will be simmering, spiced and overwhelming, cumin, smoked paprika and then small pockets in the tomato sauce, slowly poaching eggs, tons of feta and parsley.

One of the terrace doors opens slightly. Vera comes out first, followed by Gry holding Sejr. He's too big to be held like that, but not too old; he's only three but he's built like his dad. Gry's cheeks are ruddy from carrying him around. She is wearing jeans and one of her hand-knitted sweater vests and her tangled hair is everywhere; she's beautiful. She puts Sejr down, her hands on her hips.

'Should I bake some bread?'

'Yes, chef!'

Their direct communication is a good habit. Adam reaches over to give her calf a squeeze. They nod in silent agreement: they are formidable, magnanimous. Gry set up the bread before she went to bed. She used yeast, but it's fine, their starter is back home. The dough is supple from proofing in the refrigerator overnight; she's followed this recipe hundreds of times. Mustard is her secret ingredient, at once familiar and intriguing, plus a little cup of strong coffee, a few handfuls of pistachios; that's the trick: when you cut a slice, the slivers sparkle green and purple, emeralds in the jazzed-up loaf.

Gry pours the remaining coffee into a mug, brings it out to Adam who is bent over the fire, sautéing onions; he takes a sip; life is good, steam rising from the mug, from the pot.

Gry takes Vera and Sejr to the edge of the forest to pick gooseberries, which they scatter over a large bowl of yogurt, streamed with honey; she discreetly takes a few pictures on her phone of the gooseberry bushes, the pot, the lake, the smoke; of Adam, the children, creating an Instagrammable tableau. Just look at us.

Back inside, Sylvia is up; in bloomers, a loose

button-down shirt, teased hair from the night. She hugs Gry when she comes inside without a second thought, giving in to the effusiveness of the morning. They feel a childish delight, surprised to find each other here, in this house, together again. How rare it is to see each other in the morning; for years they've been meeting for coffee in the afternoon, for dinner in the evening; always put together, dressed up. Now, here they are in their pyjamas; a hint of a hangover, which they apparently get from nothing now, even from a single glass, but it only makes them more open, more porous, and their hug feels like real love, not just a polite embrace. Sylvia theatrically covers a squeal with her hand, pointing at the bowl on the kitchen counter.

'No way, just regular bread! Incredible. I'm so sick of sourdough, of my bread tasting like yogurt. Haven't we moved on yet?' Sylvia says.

In fact, Gry is proud of her patient mastery of the fermentation process, of her precise drug-dealer scale; she feels like a scientist cracking the code, making the natural processes shine, but Sylvia is so happily contrarian; it feels good to get it right.

Sylvia grabs an aged, crystallised havarti cheese and Gruyère from the fridge, a jar of dark berry jam, decides to whip some butter with a few drops of buttermilk into an airy mountain, gives it a critical look and sprinkles a snowfall of flaky salt that catches the sun like crystals.

As if whipped butter isn't hipster, Gry thinks slyly.

In their wake, Charlie has resolved to making

waffles; she can feel this breakfast becoming more of a production than she has the energy for. This friendship group, they love showing off, firing up a nonchalant, braggy brunch, eager to impress, pretending they just threw something together. Of course, they would never say 'brunch' because that would sound too passé. She considers calling their brunch a brunch out loud, just to see their barely contained excitement collapse, but she's not that petty.

Leave them to it. If anyone asks, the waffles are for the kids, but this is secretly her favourite breakfast, with melted butter and maple syrup; she knows what she likes – happy American carbs. She's ravenous in the morning; if it was up to her they would have eaten hours ago. She does think it is way too early for a stew, but she doesn't say anything, she doesn't have to.

Sylvia cringes: why does Charlie have to be so juvenile, so middle class, insisting on her rural school-kid appetite. Does she want Cornflakes too? Can't Charlie just pretend to like sophisticated things until she likes them, like other adults? Sylvia has spent the past eight years learning to love coriander (and she still doesn't like it, but at least she pretends to).

Sylvia and Gry go outside to set the table beneath the umbrella – a linen tablecloth, white and chartreuse checked, small coffee cups. They nod conspiratorially, without needing to say that the ideal they are aiming for is a shamelessly charming tablescape, maybe from a French summer film; Sylvia relaxes, she feels in tune, understood, like she and Gry are speaking the same language. She wraps her arms around Gry from behind, whispers in her ear:

'Rohmer, right?'

And while Gry finds it kind of annoying that for Sylvia everything has to be a symbol, a reference to something else – can't she just be present? – she also loves being part of Sylvia's overthought, overwrought world, feeling the anticipation brimming over the breakfast table and herself.

'Should we have goat's cheese too?' Sylvia asks.

'Don't we say *chèvre*?' Gry corrects her.

Sylvia mimes being stabbed in the heart with a huge smile. Nothing feels as tender as a precise jab – Gry seeing through her Francophilia, one-upping her. Sylvia has never loved her more.

Sejr hangs on Gry, peers up at Sylvia.

'Why are your boobs bigger than my mum's? Why aren't you wearing a bra?'

Gry covers her face. She stays in the moment, responding instead to Sylvia over his head.

'Oh honey, don't be so bourgeois.'

Sejr looks confused. Sylvia giggles.

'All boobs are different,' Gry says in a more patient, adult voice.

Through the terrace doors, Sylvia sees Quince standing in the kitchen, in thin summer pyjamas; in other words, more dressed than usual. He looks like a sweet, lost aristocrat; he'll never inherit Brideshead,

Sylvia thinks. In fact, Quince is ruffled because he just woke up and the breakfast table is already set. Now, he has to figure out his contribution, something to match the unspoken hype gathering around the endeavour. Something creative but nonchalant, something they'll go crazy for.

. . .

Of course!

Quince feels the dew, the grass, the soft pine needles. He walks past the fire pit where Adam is showing Vera how to build a fire, how to keep it going, leaving room between the kindling so the flames get enough oxygen. He adjusts the log Vera has carefully placed in the pit.

A benign scene, but also a display of authority, a demonstration of feeling at home in the world. For a guy like Adam, there's nothing better than having kids – the responsibility of raising them right, the limitless opportunities for mansplaining, Quince thinks as he approaches a lone elder tree. He picks a few handfuls of flowers; the yellow-white dust lands on the fabric of his pyjamas.

Before returning to the house, he mentally prepares himself. Should he say something to Adam when he walks by? Should he try to seem aloof? He's annoyed to even be thinking about it, aware that he is trying to live up to a masculine ideal, that he, unlike Adam, is performing his gender. But no, he corrects himself: he's a recent settler; he has staked out his own small, humble patch of the great, strange continent that is

Masculinity; he can sow and reap what he pleases. At the same time, he wants to respect the Earth, their territory. He doesn't want to fall foul of the indigenous people, he would rather learn from them. You can say a lot about cis men, but they were here first, and you, he, has to respect that.

But now the metaphor is becoming weird and fuzzy, so he does what his therapist has told him to do, open his senses – what does he feel? He is walking in soft, wet grass, with elder blossoms pressed to his body, to the thin, crispy linen of his pyjama shirt, to the chest begging to see the sun, to the ribcage emptied of years of pressure, to the heart that is lighter but still on guard, especially when some guy is building a competent fire right there in front of you.

Quince decides on a brief moment of eye contact, an amicable expression, no smile. Men nod up when they know each other well and down when they don't. He read that on a Reddit thread. Quince doesn't nod; he doesn't know what his and Adam's level of intimacy is.

When Quince enters the kitchen, he stands by Charlie, his refuge. He falls gratefully under her wing, the warmer form of stability she radiates. Like an old oak, kind but masculine too. He wonders: How does she so easily pass for male? When she isn't even trying to. And what is he, what kind of flamboyant tree? He remembers sitting under a quince tree in the King's Garden, blooming in spring, slow, pompous and pink, the petals the colour of thin skin with delicate veinlets, joined by a tight, pointy bud. The autumn fruit smelled exquisite. That was his tree.

He looks down at his elderflowers.

He feels an affinity with them too. If he was a dryad, a spirit, he would live in an elder tree, weightless among the ribbed branches: elder, which can't decide whether it wants to be a tree or a bush, no single trunk but a labyrinth, he thinks happily.

He melts some butter in the pan, adds a splash of oil, pulls Charlie's bowl of waffle batter to him, asks courteously:

'May I?'

Something in Charlie loosens, settles; now she is part of it, now there is room for her in this perform-ance the others are putting on. Quince dunks his elder-flowers in batter, drops them into the foaming brown butter and fries them into crispy bouquets.

The bread is in the oven; Gry has plaited the dough into long, twisted flutes, sprinkled flour over them, and now the crusts are dark, speckled white and ridged like bark. A magnificent spread. Adam shouts that the eggs are almost ready; will someone wake up Esben and Karen?

'We're up!'

They step onto the deck like a royal couple, and it's all worth it, to see them overwhelmed, the breakfast table a frieze in the shade, in the sun. They settle into their roles as an awestruck audience; mild, grateful regents. Esben looks at the table, takes stock – is there an *i* to dot? He goes back inside, returns holding champagne and fruit juice, bottles dewy with cold.

*

Vera builds a tower of waffles mortared with yogurt, sky-high, almost tipping. Quince appreciates how laid-back Gry and Adam are as parents, that the kids are allowed to play with their food.

'You're so talented! What a beautiful arrangement, like something you'd get at a real restaurant,' he tells Vera.

Gry looks at Vera's plate, commends:

'I see you've made an effort, honey. What are you building?'

Then she turns to Quince and adds, her voice lowered and serious:

'We always try to tell them that they've made an effort whenever they're drawing or making something. We describe what we see them doing, so they feel seen. But we don't say beautiful, because then we're praising them, which means we're evaluating them. And then they'll learn to seek our praise. Instead, we ask them questions. It's best if they can give themselves that recognition.'

Adam glances at Vera's project.

'Manners, please,' he says.

Quince's fried elder blossoms are spread over a deep blue dish. They crackle, crisp and fatty. Karen lets out a small moan, looks at Quince enrapt.

'You're making these every day!'

She says it like an order. She is always so direct, easy to love with her confident commands.

'Here, try one – you're the master chef after all!' Karen says to Gry, who loves Karen's big-sister mannerisms, feels seen, but also feels like a boring housewife. It's hard not to feel inferior. She hasn't eaten any carbohydrates for three weeks, so she could be more relaxed here. She takes note of how much Karen is eating and puts a little less on her plate.

'And you, Esben,' Karen says.

He grabs a blossom, scoops it into his mouth. Quiet falls over the table; they are always a little reverent around Esben; his opinion matters, even about deep-fried flowers.

'Insane,' he admits.

Quince revels in the praise.

'Charlie helped too,' he says modestly, and Charlie smiles shyly. Adam leans across the table to take one, bites into it and shrugs.

'They're kind of cloying, no?'

Quince's eyebrows lift above his sunglasses:

'Well, you can just take another scoop of your . . . tomato soup?' He waves in the general direction of the shakshuka. 'I'm sure that's perfectly fine.'

Karen clears her throat. They look up. She puts her palms on the table; they settle down, waiting for her to speak. Quince suppresses the urge to yell that Adam started it.

But Karen is not reprimanding anyone.

'Actually, we have a little surprise,' Karen smiles at them all. She touches her teaspoon, drawing it out, at ease in her own artful pause. A gentle breeze rustles the birch trees, the leaves shimmer chaotically in the sun. Karen continues with a reserved smile, calm:

'We've invited my family and Esben's to join us Saturday, and a few of our friends. Our *other* friends. Because . . . we're getting married!'

The breakfast scene explodes in congratulations. Gry feels the pride swelling in her, that she was the only one let in on the secret.

'Seriously?! Congrats!' Quince's jaw drops. He's thrilled. Finally, something out of the ordinary is happening, even though Karen and Esben were obviously going to get married sooner or later, but this could be a party for the ages, a mythological event.

'Amazing! What do we need to do? What can we help with? What a shame, I didn't pack anything fancy enough to wear to a wedding!' Charlie is ebullient, she loves romance, love, weddings on principle. She can't wait to have her turn with Sylvia.

It will just be a small ceremony, a dinner party, Karen clarifies.

'My whole family lives around here, so they can just stop by.'

Sylvia is frozen, her hand covering her mouth; she blinks. Gry takes her other hand, gives it a squeeze.

'Babes, are you crying?'

Sylvia nods, smiles, waves her hand as if to say

no, don't pay any attention to me. I'm just being silly, getting sentimental like this.

'Congratulations,' she whispers, weakly, almost hyperventilating, and the others laugh. Sylvia is always so dramatic.

*

Behind her sunglasses Sylvia is beside herself. They're getting married. Her chest is on fire. What the hell. But it doesn't mean anything, she tells herself; it doesn't make a difference for people like them, whether they're married or not. Not like in the old days when a wedding confirmed a couple for eternity.

And yet it does mean something. Because Esben is Esben, a limerence, a crush she has always had and keeps coming back to, even though he keeps drifting further from her. This is how it starts. First, they'll get married, just like everyone else, and soon they'll be having kids. How is she supposed to be here, pretending to be relaxed and holding her girlfriend's hand, pretending to be happy for them? She's enraged at Esben – he knows, he must know, there is something between them. They've never spoken about it, but they've always been close. All these years, they've been at each other's sides, confiding in one another. Why hasn't he ever said anything; why hasn't she?

When she thinks of the old days, she thinks of him, in a dingy pub, hundreds of nights, shrouded in smoke, how well it suited him; the shoddier his surroundings, the brighter he shone, at the table with his beer and his cheekbones, talking about whatever book he was reading, at once so animated and restrained; he could control his excitement, sublimate it.

They did sleep together once. But nothing sexual happened, they just slept. That was part of the magic, how innocent it was. They had all been to a party in his dormitory, and she and Esben had abandoned the dancefloor, found a sofa, and they talked and talked, finishing each other's thoughts. He showed her some of his own writing, a poem that he was planning to submit to a literary magazine; she tried to say something thoughtful, clever, serious about it. Eventually, the party died out, and they were the only ones left. On the sofa, she thought: *Now*, I'm grown up – *finally*, my life is sophisticated. It felt so natural to stay, to follow Esben to his room, to listen to him falling asleep; everything was so exciting and ambiguous. She lay in his arms, hearing his heartbeat slow. She woke up early in his bed, in his single white monk's room in the dorm, to a summer day like this one; the walls, the curtains, the sheets, everything was bright. She went to the open window, leaned over the deep sill and stared up at the blue sky. Esben slept as the light grew, and the whole scene swelled inside her: he had opened a window in her, everything felt new. She tiptoed out, cycled home, full of promise, of what?

*

The friends spread out cotton blankets, loungers, under the birch trees, in the sun, in the flickering shade. The children splash and shriek at the leeches whistling along the water's edge. Fortunately, the children can entertain themselves, so the adults finally have the time to do nothing, to talk, to think. Sylvia overhears Gry telling Karen how fantastic it is to be here, how she wishes it could always be like this, how little sense it makes to live in tiny city apartments – shouldn't we be closer to nature, taking turns cooking, watching the sunset each night? The children could play outside, we could raise them together. *It takes a village*, Sylvia hears her say – oh God, reciting that proverb that no one knows the origin of. Incredible, how hetero mums suddenly become socially conscious the second they see a lake. Does Gry even know what she's saying? Sylvia lets it go, as Gry and Karen continue to talk about child-care logistics – not about yearning, not about having an endless, stifled crush on your friend. On your friend's fiancé. What if they could actually have a conversation about how utopian their *village* could be?

They sprawl out, interspersed, chatting with closed eyes or sunglasses on. Adam is lying at a slight remove on his tablet, checking the news, gathering his daily overview of how the world is going to hell.

He half-follows Gry and Karen's conversation. He doesn't feel like talking about the reality of family life, even though it would make sense to do things differently, to be more collaborative. He and Gry and all the other new parents they know are completely exhausted, but what can you do, that's just how it is. At least for now. Eventually, the kids will be older, and they'll be able to do as they please. But for now, it's easier to be around people who are in the same place, who know the sleep-deprived nights, the routines and the boredom, so they retreat into their date nights and playgrounds, echoing each other's complaints. He knows he is destined for more than what his everyday life in Copenhagen currently offers him, but he doesn't mind waiting. He patiently endures the quotidian, the parallel apartments, young parents in identical Scandinavian outfits. Entire wardrobes from ARKET, mid-range and anonymous. But for now who cares, it is summer – they're in the country and the children are looking after themselves. For the first time in years, he notices the air he's breathing: still, grass and pine, sunscreen. He feels restless, a bit allergic. Tomorrow he'll go for a run – he can finally finish the book he's been reading, and make something of the time.

Quince is lying in the middle of the heap; he gazes up at the treetops looking down at them all, content – this is how it should be: intermingled bodies, a chaste, lazy orgy. Just look at how beautiful they are: loafing, lazing, Romanesque. Why did they stop making furniture for lounging, he wonders, exasperated – isn't it obvious how well it suits their bodies to stretch, to sprawl? Wouldn't the energy be better, more relaxed, or maybe not relaxed but flirty, if they could be half-lying around the table at a dinner party? If the chair had never replaced the chaise-longue. Why don't we repose more? When he thinks of the world outside the forest, he pictures hard wooden dining sets, office chairs, stiff manifestations of ergonomic puritanism and loneliness.

Quince closes his eyes. In the village church where he used to sing as a child, there was a relief of the Last Supper on the altarpiece. In the Roman Empire, in the Middle East, the apostles would have *lain* around the table – Jesus and Judas spooning in drapey robes, a *fabulous* scene. He had registered it back then, even before he had the vocabulary. Even still, he pictures them as star-crossed lovers – why else would Judas have kissed Jesus after betraying him? Why be so extra – couldn't he just have pointed? Back then, his fantasies were already grasping for something that was sinful and different and inexpressible in a girl's body. In the choir, as he sang with the other altos, he imagined himself as a Catholic altar boy, a young priest's indecent eyes on him, whipping up daydreams that bordered on perverse – even though this was a Protestant church in the Danish provinces, far from the Vatican, without any choirboys in their lovely nightgown cassocks in the nave, no incense or golden threads. His fellow choristers wore baggy sweatshirts, nondescriptly blue. Nothing unseemly ever happened, but a boy could dream.

The reeds, the rushes barely move – the air is still, but the lake exhales a cool breath. At the edge of the tableau,

Gry is keeping an eye on the kids. The water is shallow a long way out, so they can reach the bottom. She becomes aware of herself watching the kids, glances at her friends instead. They are interlaced but each of them is distinct. They resemble a relief: Karen, resting her head on Esben's thigh; Sylvia, hanging on Charlie; Sylvia's dark, wet mermaid hair stuck to her body, reaching down to her waist; Quince rubbing sunscreen onto his chest.

Now that they finally have the time to talk, Gry feels like she doesn't really know what to say. These friends she used to be so close to, they have taken many steps forward in their lives. They've become other people, or they've become more themselves. They're still young, but they are more gnarled too, less eager to please, less concerned with fitting in, saying the right thing, than they used to be in their early twenties. They've become zealous, zesty adults. Big mouthfuls. Maybe with the sole exception of herself, she thinks. She still has some of that sweetness, something girlish about her, that impulse to smooth things out, to clear the table, to remember to ask questions. Is she too trustworthy? She isn't eccentric, or maybe she is but not in the same loud way as the others. Not like Sylvia. Gry had thought the thing with Charlie, with women, was a phase, but they've been together for three years now. And Quince. Gry isn't sure what words to use about him. Do you say trans man or transmasculine or just trans? Nonbinary? Is it better not to say anything? Is it too late to ask? She wouldn't want to be offensive, or to seem out of touch.

Were she and Quince ever close, or were they just used to seeing each other every day?

Gry feels benignly stuck in this new phase of life. Shuttling between home and the office, family and academia. Maybe she is just good at it? She threads herself into and out of her maternal role, her university affiliation – she likes referring to herself as an academic, insisting on learning something new each day, on thinking abstractly, before she has to pick up the kids. Currently, she is researching aquatic plants, Nordic folklore. She loves her spot in the library, the driftwood-grey desk, the cool, dry air that clears her mind. She enjoys speaking with her colleagues, helping them with their research. She walks to the kids' preschool each day because if she cycles, the transition is too abrupt – her thoughts don't have the chance to settle before she has to be a mother again. Now, Vera and Sejr are playing in the lake, entirely safe. Vera gathers a little bouquet of aquatic plants. Gry remembers loving them as a child too: the young, light green stalks wavering in the sunlight beneath the surface, weightless, almost luminescent; the disappointment of plucking them from the water, their soggy wilting.

Her thoughts are far from the children, her work, the others, when Quince pokes her arm: Could she help him with his back? She feels happy to be asked, makes room on the blanket and he sits cross-legged with his back to her. He's tanned and warm. She feels a sudden electric charge in her fingertips, remembering how physical they all used to be, how natural it was to share a bed. Now, touching each other feels foreign and intimate. When did we stop holding hands, leaning on each other? She squints at the others, her heap of friends – maybe she's the only one who stopped?

Gry concentrates on Quince's back, the sunscreen; she's curious too, can't help noticing the musculature, the breadth of his shoulder blades. When was the last time she touched another man besides Adam? Of course, Quince is an old friend, but he's also new. His deeper voice, the way his face has become his own. She doesn't see him often – months go by, half a year, so his metamorphosis has been even clearer; each time they see each other, he's a little more at ease and aloof and radiant. It is difficult to connect the present Quince to the tall, awkward, friendly but slightly indistinct figure she used to know. Gry tries to remember the body he had before, shrouded in baggy clothes, sweatshirts in the summer heat. Hunched shoulders to make his chest more concave, or is she projecting? Is the body she's touching right now so different? Can she feel a difference – know what it is, what it signifies? Was his skin softer back then? She wonders if she is being inappropriate, invasive, by trying to feel how he's changed. But at the same time, she is also just touching a friend after a chasm of years. Something in her throat tightens.

Maybe it's not so bad that we've drifted apart, she thinks, now we can get close again? Maybe Quince would be happy to know I see him as a new person, without the palimpsest of the person I used to know?

Gry readies herself, cautiously asks: How did Quince choose his name?

'I wanted to be called something delightful. Even though Quince isn't on the official name register. I wanted something gender neutral, but the standard unisex names can feel kind of forced.'

Quince adds, half aloud over his shoulder:

'No offence, Charlie.'

Quince smiles, eyes roguishly hidden behind his sunglasses. Charlie gives him the finger from the other side of the blanket landscape, a loving gesture; their relationship has always been easy.

Quince leaps up, kisses Gry's hand in thanks (no big deal for him, Gry thinks, he's not shy about physical contact), and tousles Charlie's hair.

Charlie was a nickname that stuck. One night Charlie, Sylvia and Quince were watching *Dead Poets Society* and they agreed that she looked like Charlie Dalton, the cheekiest of the boys. Charlie likes the boyishness of her borrowed name, how it sounds like a broad grin. She likes how strong, beautiful, Sylvia makes her feel. Sylvia, who, at the start of their courtship, with her well-intentioned political correctness, asked about pronouns, whether Charlie identified as a certain gender, or . . . um, a woman. She was sulky, hurt. The question echoed thousands of days at school, stung; the broad shoulders, her sharp jawline, short hair – are you a boy or a girl? But it was healing too, how Sylvia swooned over her boyishness, couldn't get enough of her shoulders, being lifted up. She started wearing sweaters that accentuated the strength, the breadth of her back, instead of camouflaging it. Something protective flared up inside her, as if she had been waiting all this time for a fragile, nervy woman to take care of.

Quince takes hormones, rubs a magical salve over his thighs. He can more accurately dose the testosterone that way, hold back a little bit, compared to injecting it. He thinks of it as a conjuring cream. Testosterone is an upper, a joyful surprise that makes him feel like a golden retriever, happier in his body, in his life, than he's ever been. He wonders, trying not to be envious, what about Charlie's natural composition of hormones makes her so effortlessly readable as a man. But who cares, he reminds himself with a sigh of relief: he is too now. Now, when he makes a scene, he is read as gay, not girly.

He feels the willing growing pains in his muscles, but if he and Charlie were to arm wrestle (God forbid, they would *never*), Charlie would win. So at ease in the natural strength of her body; it suits her.

Her raw strength, and at the same time, her insistent vanity. Quince will forever be jealous of her wardrobe: the black denim jacket embroidered with light lavender flowers, an expensive limited edition, *Levi's dad trucker fit*. Charlie told Quince the price, but not Sylvia, who would have been scandalised. That is one of their less serious conflicts: Charlie loves quality, design, whatever the cost. When she falls, she falls hard – 17,000 kr. is perfectly reasonable for a vintage Børge Mogensen sofa with the original red-and-blue checked woollen uphol-stery. A bargain! Meanwhile, Sylvia calls herself a com-munist, even though she has not read a single word of political theory. She votes loyally for the Red/Green Alliance, but always for the party since she doesn't know any of the candidates. She never bothers with the first pages of the paper, skips straight to the culture section. In reality, Quince thinks, it is not the ideology of Charlie's materialism that bothers her but rather her unwavering, purposeful love – of an oak night-stand, of a pastel-blue fridge from the fifties, the hand-painted Koinobori streamers from Japan flying over the houseboat – which reminds Sylvia of Charlie's love for her: simple, stable, enveloping. I want you and only you. Quince has lost count of how many times Sylvia has collapsed dramatically into his lap, questioning their relationship – Charlie is so wonderful, she should be happy, but why isn't she happy-happy? Is this right for her?

Just look at her! Quince wants to shout.

What does Charlie look like? A pretty boy, no, a *soft butch*, a dream in a chunky silver necklace, a nineties Leonardo DiCaprio with a dirty-blonde centre parting, hair falling into her eyes. Quince *has* joked about her fuckboy-hair, but lovingly, and only because nothing could be further from the truth. Charlie doesn't have a Don Juan impulse in her.

Sometimes, Quince is tempted to flirt with Charlie. He gets curious when he sees her grab the nape of Sylvia's neck with a grin, when Sylvia dreamily gossips about how rough Charlie can be, how good it feels to be put in your place, taken. Quince would like to explore his and Charlie's staggered spots on the androgyny spectrum; their boyishness isn't the same but it is similar enough to be exciting; they would fight for control (he would love losing) – and Sylvia would be fine with it, he knows, but Charlie would be horrified. She is such a dirty fantasy and yet so innocent.

Quince wishes Sylvia would just relax, enjoy Charlie's faithfulness. Sylvia thinks so much, and yet she's so dumb, doesn't understand that you can't want something you already have. That she needs the security that Charlie gives her, and that she takes it for granted.

If they broke up, Sylvia would implode from the heartache and the lack of attention. She isn't like Quince, who thrives on being free.

Sylvia pokes Quince as he tells her off in his head.

'But it was also because Quince is a minor character in *A Midsummer Night's Dream*, right?'

'Of course.'

Quince smiles. But it was also just, it was just the right name. It was exactly him.

*

Sylvia and Esben follow the path away from the house, under the light green shadows of the beech trees, looking for somewhere for the guests to pitch their tents. Esben is wearing pink-tinted sunglasses. He puts an arm around Sylvia. The weight feels nice. She rests her head on his shoulder, lets her desperate thoughts sink to the bottom of her consciousness. She can come back for them later. Right now, she just wants to be here with him.

With Esben, Sylvia doesn't try as hard to *seem* clever. She tries to be genuine, to match his seriousness. But it's difficult. She wants to be unmediated, *real*, but she also wants to impress him, to say something that will make him light up. If she's being honest, she only wants to be unmediated to impress him. An ordeal. Trying to serve up her soul, as finely diced as possible.

They reach a large, open clearing, enclosed by trees: dense layers of beech, spruce sweating resin; the scent of massive Scots pines rises with the sun, the lake aglitter in the distance.

It's almost offensive, how perfect it is. He will make such a beautiful groom.

And yet, it isn't too bitter for her. She can endure the tension, day in and day out. Where does it begin, her crush? In herself, in him? It has been so long, she barely knows what it means anymore, only that she is somehow attached to him and that at times the feeling becomes all-consuming.

'What more could you ask for? This is a midsummer

extravaganza. They have to camp here. The kids can pick wild strawberries like in some Swedish film. It will be brilliant. Everyone will probably hate you a little,' she adds brightly. Okay, maybe she's trying to be a bit clever.

He pauses before answering, his eye twitching in that way she knows so well.

'I hope not, but I suppose we will have to risk it.'

He is so earnest. She used to think his thoughtful pauses were an expression of some natural gentleness but they are self-imposed. A deep-set, practised caution. How he filters everything before he speaks.

She lowers her voice: 'Is your mum coming?'

She used to be the only one who knew. How Esben's mother had been in and out of psychiatric care during his childhood, the impact it had on him. Sylvia has held onto all his secrets like a parent keeps their child's teeth. He is so controlled that each confession feels so rare and valuable. But now he's told the world everything, with his book, and she is only slightly disappointed.

Esben has always let Sylvia read his writing before it is published. Even though she tries her best to be objective, professional, everything he shows her is a chance to see inside him. She remembers the first time, sensing his shyness, starting with three comments about metaphor before posing her real question, straining to seem casual: Is this inspired by your own life? She had coaxed and coaxed.

And she discovered that Esben suspects that he

has something inside him, the same force, the same current, as his mother. He doesn't want to find out if he would fall, if he wouldn't – instead, he respects his fear of heights, takes precautions, only drinks in moderation, exercises regularly, even though he doesn't enjoy it, takes days off, making sure the water stays calm; he is the only thing in the world he has control over.

Sylvia agrees that he has it too, offshoots of whatever it was that grew too large and difficult for his mother. He has an intensity that he won't let surface, let speak. Tempestuous gusts that could tear him open, those late nights, when they had all been out, drinking red wine, talking and talking, and Esben, who was usually so reserved, would start interjecting, making bold proclamations that were almost prophetic, persuasive, but bordering on incomprehensible. After those kinds of outbursts, he retreats. Out of embarrassment, but also to write.

Sylvia is touched by his heroic, dogged energy, the pains he takes. He could so easily have lost his way, become someone shouting in the middle of the street, conversing with God at a red light; instead he has become the most successful of them all. He doesn't come from money, from security – it wasn't a given that he'd manage his psyche as he's done. His steely softness, his disciplined writing practice – it's easy to overlook because he is so discreet, but he is ambitious, has something strong and enduring in him that has enabled him to write three books.

She doesn't love him *because* he has been nominated for literary prizes, or because he, out of shyness and on principle, refuses to be interviewed, but she is vain enough to take pleasure in being so close to an introverted celebrity, knowing him as a person, that he has chosen her as his confidante.

He responds in his usual considered way.

'Yes, my mum is coming. She's in a good place. Thank you for asking.'

He pulls her into a hug. His embrace cracks something open in her, a fissure of light. She feels weightless, doesn't dare move.

He inspects the edge of the forest, his arm still wrapped around her, and smiles – neither of them are botanists; they don't know what kinds of trees they're looking at. For them, the smell of resin, the patches of light on the forest floor, are purely aesthetic, cinematic. She sneaks a glance at him.

Esben looks tremendous under the speckled shadows of the trees; his sharp features, those stubborn Huguenot genes that have been repeating the same range of colours for five centuries, that pale complexion, quick to blush, since the French Renaissance. His ancestors were that kind of Protestant guerrillas. She wonders if the inherited, dogged wildness in him is related to the fanatic kind of passion that emboldened a small, reformed minority to wage a multi-century war against Catholicism, even though they were outnumbered eight times over, sacrificing themselves to one massacre after another, bloodbath after bloodbath. But Sylvia reckons he would never mythologise his origins in that way.

'Should we pick some flowers?'

The fireweed bakes in the sun, an upright coral reef, flower sceptres, pink and purple, tons of them. Sylvia likes that Esben isn't afraid to seem feminine. They break off the stems close to the ground, to keep them long so the bouquet will be lavish, imposing, arranging the fireweed and jubilant bluish-purple lupins. They move deeper into the forest, following the flowers along the path.

Then Esben grabs her shoulders, points, whispering: 'Look, in there!'

The path leads them to a secret, oval grove. They wade into the miracle. This has to be the most beautiful clearing in the whole forest. The fir trees tower around them, tall as church walls, dark green and ceremonial, the branches bound with honeysuckle, their blossoms still closed, curry yellow and warm violet, small firework explosions, frozen in time, and everywhere elder is in bloom, yellow-white umbels bright and weighty, a flowering chalk painting. The crown of a majestic oak spreads open at the bottom of the clearing, like the altar of a pagan nave.

Sylvia buzzes. Jackpot. This is perfect. It smells incredible. If they don't throw themselves into each other's arms, if nobody does, it's a waste of the most picturesque midsummer scenery. Everything in the forest inhales with her, quickening her breathing. She walks over to the oak tree, looks up at its branches, its gnarled and regal crown, trying to be understated, like Esben. He follows her, stands behind her. Breathes.

'A church of the forest,' Sylvia whispers, and immediately tenses. Was that too melodramatic, or was it just right?

'And just think that we found this place together!'

Esben looks around.

'It's so intimate here, so portentous, so . . . steep,' he says, with a wave of his hand, as if steepness was the most significant quality of the grove. Sylvia notices the red blotches on his neck, by his temples, that appear whenever Esben gets worked up.

He asks, hopefully:

'Should we have the ceremony here?'

'We have to,' Sylvia agrees, slipping into his 'we', feeling significant, as if this forest church is hers to give. She offers it to him on the spot. She might be greedy, but she isn't stingy.

'C'mon. We have to show everyone else.'

Sylvia is gleeful at the thought of her and Esben returning to the house, marching in like proud children arriving from a faraway adventure, with bright eyes, shields of purplish flowers at their chests. When they tell them about the forest church, the others will *have* to be envious, will have to admit that their friendship is special. That they have something in common, that she makes him happy. Right now, he doesn't look like someone who has ever been tempestuous.

*

Gry is knitting by the lake. Her ball of wool has run out, so she takes another from her bag, pauses for a moment. She sits, looking into the distance. Charlie crouches down next to her.

'Can I show you a trick?' Charlie asks.

'Of course.'

'This is wool, right?'

'*High*-quality wool,' Gry responds, cheekier than usual.

Charlie spits into her palm. She takes the threads from Gry's knitting and from the new ball of wool and rubs them together between her hands. When she opens her hands the two threads have become one. She tugs it a little, rolls it between her fingers; it holds.

'The enzymes in the spit hold the fibres together. It's called spit splicing.'

Charlie looks up.

'Sorry, it's a bit gross,' she says.

'No, it's genius,' Gry says.

Now Vera and Sejr are wading back in; they run up to the blanket, beg Gry to come in with them. She insists they play on their own, that it's good for them.

And Gry likes Charlie. She wants to stay in the moment with her. She wishes they saw each other more. But it's difficult to find the time with Sylvia, with

Quince too. They don't understand what it's like having kids, that she can't stay out late on weeknights, spontaneously go to some hip karaoke bar. She can barely get out when they make plans in advance. Sylvia was so mad the last time she cancelled because the kids were sick again. Her heavy breathing on the phone. Did Gry really hear her dump the dinner she had made into the kitchen sink? Gry had apologised profusely, but that's just how it is. Kids are always getting sick. You would know that if you knew anything about the public childcare system. Sylvia and Quince could offer to help with the kids once in a while. They see themselves as social, supportive, but in reality they are selfish.

Charlie says she'll go for a swim with the kids, and Gry is grateful, even though it goes against her parenting philosophy. Gry can't help but notice the tanned nape of Charlie's neck, the silver necklace, the muscles in her back as she pulls off her T-shirt. Charlie doesn't care for bikini tops. Could Gry be that free and naked in the water? They are all friends here after all, no one else can see them.

Charlie swims around with the kids, taking slow, easy breaststrokes. They're comfortable around her. Gry is comfortable too. There's something about Charlie, her interwoven care and strength, which is almost part of her physique. People usually fall into one of two categories, Gry thinks; either you're strong and aloof, like Adam and Karen, or you're sweeter, softer, but also a little weaker, like the rest of them. But Charlie is different, an adventure hero: steady, warm and good, that extra capacity.

Gry shuts her eyes, lets herself drift into a daydream: Charlie is a boatbuilder. She has a way with the ropes, comes home from work with streaks of oil up her arms, muscles glowing from strain; it's to die for. Gry lets the image become a warm tingle in her stomach. She puts down her knitting, gets up, goes over to Adam and lies in his shadow. Her shoulder, burning from the sun, against his makes him open his body to her. He shuts his eyes, puts an arm around her and draws her warmth to him; throws his screen onto the grass.

*

They can't stay out in the sun for too long. Inside it's pleasant, the floor tiles keep their cool: broad butter-coloured squares. Quince is sitting at the dining table, his dressing gown open, writing in a notebook; he adjusts his reading glasses.

Sylvia is sprawled out on the sofa with a book. She sinks into the ribbed, pine-green corduroy, trying to think of something other than Esben, Charlie, Karen, the wedding.

She's reading Virginia Woolf's *To the Lighthouse*, accepting her own pretentiousness. She knows her love of the novel is pure, that she reads it every single summer. For the tremble of envy at the billowing world that the Ramsay family and their summer guests inhabit. The rolling waves, the flickering light on the sand. None of the characters ever grow tired of looking at each other. Are they in love, rivals, friends, enemies? What if we could always be rocking to and fro like them, trying to encircle each other, weighing our feelings off by the gram, searching for the right words?

She recalls a lecture from her first year at university, the professor's claim that *To the Lighthouse* illustrates the historicity and demise of the Victorian family. And how she, back then, stubborn and irritated had thought to herself: Are you serious? This book is about feelings, desire.

She enjoys the stream of consciousness; she appreciates a well-placed semicolon, but she doesn't read books for literary techniques. She would never in her life read a book as an example of modernism but always for its instructions on how to live: that it is possible to fling yourself at someone's feet, put your head to their knee and weep because you love them so much, because you are overwhelmed by beauty, by love, by the lake house (well, no, Lily Briscoe actually thinks: Alas, why can't you rest your face in someone's lap and declare your love on a regular afternoon; she resists, but she wants to).

This disappointment haunts her, that her friends don't believe in books, in movies, in fiction, in the same way she does. Back when she was at university, she took the reading seriously, too literally. She wasn't preparing for her exams – she was preparing for life. She still is. Every book opens a potential new world, new forms of life. Something to strive for, to inhabit.

When Sylvia makes a table arrangement with lemons and stone fruits, she's not just copying the al fresco dinners in *Call Me By Your Name*. She doesn't just want it to look like a film, it's supposed to *be* like a film. Where you can let yourself be torn adrift by love, where you can enter another space (she looks at the door to the room where Karen and Esben are sleeping: over it, a wet towel is hung up to dry, and in her mind the towel's red Greek pattern is a gate, a warning, a representation of everything that can't happen). She sighs.

Adam enters the room, flops down on the other end of the sofa, and Sylvia sits up to make room for him. He has a book in his hand too.

'What are you reading?' she asks.

'It's a travelog about Europe's lost generation.'

Sylvia bites her lip – she's not great with dates.

'Is that around . . . the beginning of the twentieth century?'

'No, it's us,' Adam responds, straightening up.

Sylvia laughs, delighted. How satisfying to be seen, acknowledged.

Adam squints to read the title of her book, makes a face.

'You're a bit of a character – you know that, right?'

Sylvia raises her eyebrows, falls quiet, waits to see whether he acknowledges his rudeness. But he is how he is: direct. He adds:

'I don't like Virginia Woolf.'

'Have you read her?'

'I've read that one.'

Sylvia is taken aback but hardly offended. She had filed Adam under the category: office manager, no soul. She feels the smile spread through her body; how charming that he reads classics, that he doesn't pretend to like them but has his own opinion. It goes along with his directness, his pragmatism, his high-quality shirts. His words have a derisive, persuasive weight, like an archetypal older brother.

'I read a lot. *To the Lighthouse* is on every list of the best novels ever written. But it is wildly overrated.'

Sylvia feels the blood prickle in her cheeks. This is her territory, and she'll fight for it. She lays the open book over her chest like armour.

'Do you want to elaborate, or should we duel at dawn?'

It feels good to argue. To meet something steadfast in one another. Sylvia senses that Adam doesn't respect her, doesn't expect much from her, thinks she's fragile, tortured. And she is. But she's also done her reading. She lets him continue.

'It's so introspective and boring. Nothing happens. It's all people looking at each other and gratuitously long sentences. The tension is completely superficial.'

'And is that not the best thing in the world?'

'The only good part is the middle, with World War I, when one of the main characters dies in a parenthetical, ice cold.'

'Well, alright, tough guy.' Sylvia is still smiling, but

her courage is sinking. She feels an affinity to precisely the hypersensitive hysteria that he is rejecting. They both think the novel is an orgy of interiority, but he finds it trivial. She scratches the pine-green corduroy with a fingernail, decides to betray her love and play on his turf. Now, she wants to impress him.

'But that is such a naïve reading, Adam. If you turn up the level of abstraction a notch, the novel illustrates a historical moment: the demise of the sanctity of the Victorian family, how the First World War results in a class society and a pragmatist ideology,' she starts, pleased to see something in Adam's face waver, intrigued, as she pontificates, reaching for the weapons he respects: argument, reason, external forces, the economy, war.

Adam looks at her expectantly, as if she might as well continue.

But then she hesitates, because she doesn't want to win this discussion by referencing world wars; she wants to return to the barb the conversation started with, to the matter of taste, of distaste, what he thinks of the novel, what he thinks about her. Most of all, she wants to get behind his armour, talk her way closer to him – they've known each other for seven years now, and she is familiar with his professional complaining about his job at the ministry, the state of the world, his children, but he never says a word about his inner life. Probably, he likes to imagine that he doesn't have an inner life.

Or maybe she is just imagining he has one?

'But is it just because you're so . . . hard, that you don't like it?'

'What do you mean by hard?'

She forces herself not to back down, hopes he respects shameless flirting, repeats:

'Just that, *hard*. No, I mean: Because you understand yourself as a doer. Facing the external world. Like some kind of Sartrean existentialist: it doesn't matter what you think or feel, only what you do.'

He leans back on the sofa.

'I don't like Sartre either.'

She sighs, performatively resigned. Is he being ironic, self-ironic? He rubs his eyes, he is being provocative, but he *is* well-read, *has* a real opinion about everything. He's not just trying to wind her up. It takes everything she has to keep her mouth shut.

'But yes,' he continues. 'If I'm going to read a novel, then I want the brutal, American detective version of existentialism. That genre has a more interesting, French-American history than you might expect. You know, Bogart read Sartre, and Sartre watched Bogart's movies. And Camus even dressed like Bogart. It's a long story, I can recommend a book on it. But anyway, the worldviews are the same: the hero is the existential cowboy. We are all doomed to freedom and that is all there is. With the detective antihero running around in a meaningless reality in which the old mores have fallen away, and he needs to *do* something, just try something, see if it works, see what happens.'

Sylvia couldn't care less about an American take on French philosophy, or the other way around, but it suits her just fine that he is talking so much. He is talking fast now, his tone is didactic.

'It's not about feelings, not even about thinking – action is all that counts. Making the most of your freedom.'

Sylvia attempts to sound both snide and cute:

'You're such a cliché. You wish you were walking around in a trench coat, ready to fight.'

'Ha! Better that than some feelings orgy,' Adam retorts as he gets up, athletic, is through the back door and out in the sunlight in a few paces. Sylvia feels heavy and floaty on the soft green fabric. *Stay*, a voice inside her pleads in vain. She reviews the conversation in her head, how she called him naïve, a cliché. She hopes it sunk in, she wants to keep arguing. She realises she could be talked down to for hours.

If he wanted. But Adam is always on his way out the door. And in his absence, an icy realisation sinks in: he has tons of raw intellectual energy, just not for you.

Sylvia shakes it off – the rejection shifts into inspiration.

She has two thoughts.

That Adam is the kind of guy you'd have missionary sex with just to continue fighting face-to-face.

And that he is right. What she, what all of them, lack is action, just *doing something*. She doesn't want to keep lying on the sofa – she wants to get up, walk resolutely out of the house, onwards, into the world of action, but what would she do then?

At the table, Quince's chin is resting in his hand, as the pencil floats across the page in the notebook. He replays Sylvia and Adam's conversation, which he heard all of: Sylvia's restrained eagerness, Adam's droning on.

Even when you disagree with men like Adam, it is always for their sake, to please them, to impress them. And because that kind of man never says very much, their rare interjections, their considerations, are all the weightier. You want to know what they are thinking, what they have inside.

In his notebook Quince writes:

The false scarcity of male speech.

Beneath that he adds:

Don't turn into a jerk.

Quince considers. In fact, he'd make a fantastic Bogart. He's always doing things, improvising. As if Adam ever goes outside the lines.

He clears his throat, looks up from his notebook at Sylvia, takes off his glasses.

'Did he just mansplain Virginia Woolf to you?'

'It's okay,' she winks. 'Mansplaining is one of my kinks.'

*

Charlie and Karen are sitting under the birch tree, working on the seating plan. There are only a few handfuls of guests, but that doesn't make it easier. The shadowy foliage envelops them like a shawl.

'You must think we're so heteronormative. I almost can't handle the thought of being a summer bride,' Karen says, twisting her hair into a bun.

Charlie grins.

'Actually, I really want to get married. I'd love to have a big wedding.'

'Of course. It means more when you're two women, then you're making a political statement, about visibility.'

'I'm not so idealistic,' Charlie says. 'I've just always wanted to get married. And not just for the wedding. I want to be married. I want a house. The whole package.'

She has always pictured a big garden, kids running around in the spring and summer, leaping through the sprinklers; in the background, away from the house, there are hiding places. Sylvia reading on the lawn, and Charlie bringing her coffee. They could be naked in the sun, hidden by the hedges. The cookie-cutter houses, the privets, are so easy to hate, but tell me that the scent of a flowering hedge on a spring day isn't intoxicating. They could have a greenhouse, maybe a vegetable garden; they could open the back door and run out for some dill on a summer night, rhubarb, teach the kids to garden. She would take care of everything; she would insulate the house, put up shelves, stock the larder. It would all come together, with her appreciation for good-quality things, Sylvia's knick-knacks and cut-outs. She would never tell anyone, but she feels that her life only started when she met someone she could build something with, when she met Sylvia. She thinks that they were meant to be.

'Are you thinking of buying a house?' Karen asks.

'We can't afford anything in the city. I wouldn't mind moving somewhere else. Sylvia's rent is ridiculous, but she thinks that it is some kind of political statement not to own anything. Even though we're mostly on the boat. It's fine for now, but I would love to live by the water. Out of the city.'

Sylvia seems not to understand. That a house is an investment, that it gets more valuable over time, a way of saving for their kids and their kids' kids. Whenever she brings up the subject, Sylvia says something idealistic and naïve about solidarity and the housing market.

The ship is sailing off without them, and the longer they wait, the harder it will be to board. Charlie wishes they had children, but at least it will be easier to get a loan before they're born.

'It will happen,' Karen assures her.

Charlie nods, and the pictures queue up inside her: the house, the blanket by the lilacs in the garden, the coast, growing old, becoming the locals walking down to the beach in their worn bathrobes, taking a morning dip in the sea. But in reality, these external things don't matter. So long as the two of them are together. When she can snuggle up to Sylvia at night and hold her. Sylvia sleeps at her own apartment occasionally, not because anything is wrong, but sometimes she just needs a night to herself, to spread out. Charlie accepts it, but she doesn't understand it. For her, the best thing in the world is falling asleep intertwined. She doesn't mind the heat, they sleep naked with thin summer duvets, with the door open. Sylvia stands by the door, looking out at the night before she comes to bed, so beautiful with her dark hair against the canal, against the May night, the June night, the whistling birds, swallows and swifts diving through the air.

'Having a family has always been important to me,' Charlie says. 'Just wait, then you'll see heteronormativity. To be honest, I'm so tired of the queer scene, of everything needing to be alternative and fluid and radical. When you're already a minority, why make things even harder for yourself? I just want peace and quiet. I want to sit in an armchair with a good book and a cup of coffee. I want to cook. I would take the kids to the water park. Whenever I'm somewhere like here, I feel my inner dad marching in, looking for some trees to chop down for the fire. I just wish it could stir up something in Sylvia too.'

'It sounds like you're ready for retirement. That's my nightmare,' Karen says. 'I love being at work. Esben is the one who takes care of everything at home.'

Charlie nods, forgets to listen to Karen speaking. She thinks about family as a kind of investment too, a factor tree. You have two kids, maybe three, and then they have their own kids, two, maybe three, it's a matter of multiplication – then there's someone to sit by your deathbed. Morbid, she knows, but she likes the thought of being a patriarch someday, a *Godfather*, sitting in an armchair and ebbing out, old but awe-inspiring, concentric circles of progeny gathered around her like walls and moats. Sowing and sowing and sowing. Harvesting and harvesting and harvesting.

When Charlie was younger, she watched that movie about a grasshopper and some ants. It made a deep impression on her. The grasshopper sings and plays and loafs about all summer, while the ants work, building their reserves. And when autumn comes, the grasshopper keeps playing, still not taking the inevitable cold seriously, just keeps playing its violin. She always hated the scene when the grasshopper is warned but doesn't wise up, and finally winter comes and rips the leaves from the trees, and the grasshopper ends up weak in a snowdrift. Because it's Disney, the ants take pity on the grasshopper and carry it into their hill, dry it off, give it some soup. Maybe that was when she decided the ants were right; or maybe the cartoon just showed something that was already inside her; that she wanted to save up and lean into the surplus later.

She sees Sylvia coming through the door, approaching them.

When Charlie met Sylvia years ago, Sylvia stole her heart with her grasshopper ways. And something inside her felt heroic. What would have happened to Sylvia if she hadn't found her, if she hadn't saved her, if she wasn't always saving her? She feels like a prince, taking

care of Sylvia, fragile Sylvia, who doesn't understand
how the world works, who can't even drive a car.

*

Sylvia interrupts Charlie and Karen, tickles Charlie's
neck with her little finger.

'Can I borrow you for a sec?'

Luring Charlie away from the wedding planning
feels like a small victory. She hopes that Karen or Esben
or Adam will notice, will wonder what they're up to; she
snuggles up to Charlie to signal that they're up to something dirty; she feels sorry, but not sorry enough not to;
guilt is salt, it makes everything taste better, more like
itself, until suddenly there's a milligram too much and
the whole dish is ruined. Their room is cool, the white
sheets lustrous. Sylvia closes the door behind her, pulls
her dress over her head and looks up at Charlie. Charlie
kisses her shoulder, her neck, a teasing touch.

'What do you want, babe?'

Sylvia mews, feels her breath deepen, feels the conversation with Adam throbbing inside her, her heart
thumping, an old, familiar feeling bubbling, layers of
desire riling each other up. And somewhere in the
background is Esben, rattling her. What's wrong with
her? Why is she behaving like a teenage boy, ready to
be taken by whatever, whoever? She curls into Charlie,
her stronger body. Sylvia lets herself be pressed up
against the door, feels Charlie tightening her grasp on
her face as she kisses her – it feels good to be held up,

Charlie pushing aside her knickers with her other hand. Whenever they have sex, she feels how well they fit. How they're both playing pretend and are fully themselves, how they want the same thing.

'Tell me I'm stupid.'

'You're so stupid, you're such a stupid little girl,' Charlie whispers, half patronising, half consoling, as she begins to touch her.

'And so good and so wet.'

Sylvia sighs, clings to Charlie's shoulders, presses her lips together to not make too much noise, gasps anyway when Charlie turns her around and pushes two fingers into her, hard – it feels right, she's gone in the feeling of being filled up, her cheekbones against the door, warm skin against the veins of the wood. She follows Charlie's movements, resists, tries to gasp without a sound, lets it build up inside her. Charlie is pressing her face against the cool wood, it feels so good to be tense, held down. She just wants to feel Charlie's fingers, to concentrate on the feeling, but she feels her knees buckle, her thigh muscles whining – her voice comes out small and broken: can she lie down, please. Charlie pretends not to hear.

'Can I lie down, please?' she asks again. Charlie holds her mouth, fucks her harder, Sylvia can feel her smile against her ear, her feigned impatience.

'Shut up,' she whispers. 'You're so spoiled.'

The scold is a caress too, a coddle. Sylvia knows

it, and she melts, moaning through Charlie's fingers, grateful, limpid.

Charlie takes pity on her, carries her to the bed, puts her down. Licks her slowly, lets Sylvia squirm with each movement, draws it out. It feels so good, like waves crashing on the shore, water sinking into the wet sand, making it shine like mother of pearl, before the next wave crashes, white foam, shining, retracting, and the next one and the next one.

'Should I make you come?'

'May I?'

Sylvia doesn't know what Charlie does differently, but her body lets go, liquefies, the waves washing over her, bigger and bigger, lifting her up so she floats – her brain, her navel, her clit, everything bright and glistening as she comes.

She lays back, basking in the miracle: she has been a jug full of dark, heavy liquid, and now, the jug is broken, all the darkness has flowed out of her, and now she's lying here, the shards quietly collecting in Charlie's embrace, and now the jug is whole again, empty and light. This is why it has to be so hard, so she can fall apart and be riveted again. It feels like a game, and at the same time, like the most concrete form of care she's ever felt.

Charlie mumbles into her neck.

'What if we bought a place like this someday?'

It sounds so right, and it sounds totally wrong.

'Mm,' Sylvia hums, not a rejection but not a word to be taken either. They lie close together, feeling each other's skin.

Eventually, she hears Charlie's breath becoming heavy, calm. She feels time passing, the light changes. The others have probably eaten by now. She regrets missing dinner but is also pleased with her and Charlie's telling absence, the casual flex of their sex life.

She feels bad for thinking that. If only she could be present, could be in the moment. She wishes she could fall asleep, let go.

Why can't I do this? Just be in it – be happy.

She fits well with Charlie. She is flighty, and Charlie is solid. She remembers a television series where a woman said: 'In every relationship, there's a rose and a gardener.' Sylvia has never doubted that she was the wild garden, Charlie the patient gardener. That Charlie protects her, keeps her safe. It feels like being let inside, like someone's lit a fire and nothing can go wrong. But why does she feel so strange right now? As if the fire is still burning, sucking the oxygen out of the room – the heat and the safety are too much, the skin contact, lying so close together. Like on the houseboat, how it gets so claustrophobic that the smallest slosh makes her seasick, nauseous. She tries to be quiet, kicks off the duvet.

She loves Charlie. It's just the *repetition*. The intimacy, content to repeat itself until you die or split up. She finds it easiest to be alone with Charlie when they're having sex. Otherwise, she feels guilty, tries to wriggle out of her doubt. But now that Charlie is asleep, Sylvia can hear her own thoughts. She speculates about the others – are they awake in the rooms around her? Are they intertwined? She imagines Esben and Karen sleeping together – that's how she would put it, not *fucking* or *screwing*, cool but still intimate: sleeping together.

They don't say anything, but have cinematic, athletic, minimalistic sex (sweat just the right amount, blush just the right amount). The sheets are always white and ample, big enough to twist and twist without ever slipping off the mattress. Organic sex, a little serious without being self-serious. Dirty talk would never even occur to them; it would be an artsy silent film, or would look like something directed by Joachim Trier, written by Sally Rooney: tasteful, understated, naturalistic but highly photogenic.

She thinks about Gry and Adam; he probably lifts her up a lot. But otherwise she imagines their sex as pretty vanilla – Gry's mildness, her glorious, voluminous hair when she lets it down, all the innocence without a whiff of perversity. What a waste. Sylvia knows without knowing that Gry was one of those girls who French-plaited her friends' hair during break times, and if Sylvia had to generalise, she would say there are two types of women: the ones who braided each other's hair, and the ones who grew up to be kinky adults.

But Adam, with his temper – would he like it rough?

Does he need to make an effort not to be destructive? Is he an alpha male with an elfin wife, doomed to frustrating, respectful sex – is that why he also seems so grumpy? Sylvia giggles. But who knows, maybe their sex life is otherworldly; maybe Gry is a dom, a queen; what does she know? Even though all of their friends are so open and caring and love to talk about themselves, they would never dream of sharing what they do in bed, and risk breaking the irony, letting down their armour. Sylvia puts her hand out, taps her knuckles against the wall. How thin are the walls? Well, maybe the others know something now.

At least she can talk to Quince, her co-conspirator, and compare their secret notes. Quince, who walks around looking like an ad for sin, a shepherd boy from antiquity, a noble gentleman. He collects swooning femmes at Dyke Night, gets picked up on Grindr, in Amager Commons. That charisma that dances off him, that rubs off on everyone around him. She loves him for being a real Pan, a confusing forest god. She loves him for his confusion, how he can be so confident and in doubt at the same time. It only makes him more irresistible.

In confidence, he shares his ambivalence, his grappling. Oh, those genders. He still doesn't really know. He doesn't know if the testosterone gel has come to stay. He wonders if he is giving up some essential part of himself by deciding on a gender, pronouns. For him, gender is not grammar but poetry.

He has said: I like my body, I like the ambiguity. A vulva and a clit-dick that is visible but still small, lovely, a happy side-effect of the testosterone. A body carved in a Glyptotheque colonnade, a sculptor's dream, in all its modesty. Once, he told her about the statue of Hermaphroditus, reclining at the Louvre. Quince loves the myth of Hermaphroditus, the son of Hermes and Aphrodite, and the nymph who fell in love with him, melted together with him. It's an inside joke between him and Sylvia – no one says 'hermaphrodite' anymore, of course not, but maybe Quince could make it modern again. Part of him relishes being a Greek fantasy, an embodiment of what men and women have secretly gone crazy over for thousands of years. Give it five years, leave it to him – everyone will want it.

He says *he* because it feels right, but also because *he* is a concept that could use a little self-doubt. And doubt, double meanings, is something he can help with.

Sylvia remembers him once winking and saying, as if denying any loyalty to masculinity: 'Being a man today, it's like arriving late to the party. It's not even opportunism – the patriarchy is a smoking heap of rubble.'

Day 3

On the terrace, Quince unrolls a yoga mat. He stretches, illuminated by the sun in blue denim cut-offs, bends over, lifts himself up on his forearms; a flexible circus act, one leg extended straight up towards the sky, the skin of his belly and back drinking in the sunshine. He has kept himself out of the sun for a year, followed the doctor's orders, but now he won't stay inside one more day. He wants to be tanned, and if the scars on his chest lighten up instead of blending in, so what? Let them, he has nothing to hide. He's feeling good today, moving fluidly from one pose into the next. Is doing yoga in the middle of everything too much, treating the deck as a stage?

No, he doesn't mind putting on a show. In fact, it irritates him that no one is up yet – where is his audience? He woke up uneasy, couldn't go back to sleep. He never gets up early. After finishing his routine, he goes down to the lake, takes off his clothes. The surface of the water is mauve in the morning light. What a shame that no one is here to swoon over the landscape with him. The water is so calm, streaming through his fingers as he takes a few strokes, dives under, lets himself float on his back, runs his fingers through his hair, shakes out his curls, spreads them out so the cool water can reach his scalp. He still swims like a child, staying in the water for hours, weightless, fabricating underwater worlds. When he was older, he discovered the resistance of wrapping his hand around the water and moving it quickly back and forth, imagining what it would be like to have a dick. Actually, the thought didn't really appeal to him. But if he turned his hand around, that was like giving the lake, the sea, a hand job, and *that* was something. He tries it now, getting onto his knees, held up by the shallow, grey-purple water. He pumps his hand, taken by the scene: the chattering birds, the soft splashes.

He hears the quick steps of someone running at the last second. Springs off, turns his hand motions into breaststrokes.

When he looks back, Adam is standing by the shore, hands on his knees, catching his breath. Ten kilometres every morning? Of course.

'How's the water? Is it cold?'

How is Quince supposed to respond to that? Who cares about the temperature? It's idyllic here. He narrows his eyes: 'Umm. It's brisk, I guess?'

Adam turns to go back to the house. Quince is relieved for a second, but he can't help himself, he has no impulse control. He squawks, not too loud, but the implication is clear enough in the morning stillness: 'Chicken.'

Adam stops. He turns around and pulls off his T-shirt. His skin is marbled red from the run. He wades into the water in his running shorts, dives under. Adam doesn't go for a dip – he swims. Front crawl. Past Quince, who is suddenly aware of his nakedness, feeling trapped in the water, as he watches Adam swim further out. He could be out of the water by now, he can still get out, but now Adam is turning around, swimming back to the shore. He can let Adam get out first.

But then Adam stops. Treads water. Impossible to read. He turns his back to Quince, looks out at the lake. Is he waiting for me to get out? Quince doesn't understand what Adam wants. Now it's just quiet. Awkward.

Then Adam dives under the water. Quince doesn't wait to see how long he stays down; he rushes up to the shore, hops into his shorts, half runs back to the house, wanting to go back to bed, to start the day over again.

*

Gry and Karen are preparing lunch, slicing vegetables for an elaborate salad. Gry assigns Sylvia the fennel, comments on how well the children have slept; it must be the fresh air. Sylvia regrets having offered to help. Here they are in this gorgeous landscape, talking about bedtimes, sleep quality. She chops. All of these small, stupid rituals nuclear families have come up with just to complete them; doing it all, having it all, making it *work*, she can picture it. Rushing around in the morning, making breakfast, efficient bickering, hurrying out the door, reuniting on the other side of the workday, conquering the same enemies day after day: Dinner, Dishes, Bedtime.

So that they can collapse, curl up next to each other on the same grey corner sofa, one resting their head on the other's chest, calmly breathing, assuring each other that the hectic days are actually nice, yes, the meaning of life. Each day endured and managed.

Sylvia tries to listen while Gry ponders the children's dinner aloud – should they have something for dessert, maybe they can make something with the rhubarb growing behind the house?

It's not that she dislikes Gry. Or Karen.

However.

Their uncomplicated normality. Gry's hand-knitted ballerina cardigans, a whisper of alpaca, her yogini strength; Karen's zebra-print one-piece, kitsch but divine, elegant, on her, her natural slimness. Sylvia still feels awkward next to them; feeling fat is a pre-condition of surrounding yourself with friends with humanities degrees. They've always eaten cruciferous vegetables; they know how to handle an artichoke. The type that makes extravagant meals for other people and then forgets to eat. Sylvia is more likely to forget that she's already eaten and eat again. They don't shave their legs, which costs them nothing because they have soft, babyish down that shyly shimmers in the sun, not Sylvia's dark, statement hair. And just like their hair is blonde and unobtrusive, they just happen to be straight – it's easy for them, free of charge, to be themselves. They are liberal-minded, and of course, they've kissed a pretty girl at a rave in Berlin once – that goes without saying – but they've never been shouted at in the street for holding hands with their girlfriend.

They aren't judgemental or conservative. They aren't about to move to the suburbs, even though (she glances at Gry) she might soon enough (the money, the reasonable mortgage rates she's married into). Sylvia wouldn't be surprised if Gry was the first to abandon ship, charmed by some lovely, organic housing community, someplace expensive and idealistic.

No, you might mistake Gry and Karen for living conformist lives, but they and their men are tolerant, left-wing, progressive. That's what's so provocative: they get to be right, to win on both courts, unconventional but conventional, tolerant but perfectly aligned with the statistics. They keep up with contemporary, experimental literature, while taking care of their 1.5 children, adding their names to the waiting lists of their own well-managed housing cooperatives, the image of happiness in their PH-lamp-lit open kitchens, steaming bao buns.

The millennial bourgeoisie.

Has history ever produced something so perverse?

The fennel is now finely diced.

Sylvia thinks of the decade of their thirties as The Great Betrayal.

They sat in the library together. They read Foucault. They read all kinds of radical theorists who wanted to revolutionise daily life. They read consciousness-expanding poetry. They went to protests, spoke fluent social critique. They got top marks. We read Sara Ahmed; we were warned: about how the normative drive to happiness puts the nuclear family centre stage and leaves other forms of life out of its limelight. Or what? Were they just studying for their exams? Was she the only one who took it literally? You all took more drugs than me back then. Now you're so calm. Are you happy? You seem happy.

She had believed they would do something else, all of them, something more fluid. The thirties were supposed to be like the twenties, only with more money and fewer complexes. Instead, they've become more traditional, more like their parents. The only hope to their living so faithfully up to their generational statistics is that they will probably get divorced – it's just a matter of time. But until then, she will despise the musical chairs of dating, how everyone looks around, makes eye contact with someone else, so that they can make their own little cell, sit on their chairs, on their settees, and then they're set.

The boring, synchronous couples race. No one has the imagination to do anything else. Weren't they true radicals just a second ago?

The crime is not the singular, conventional couple as such, she thinks, suddenly feeling gracious, self-righteous. Rather, it is the conventional couple's total dictatorship that must be dethroned, she continues, feeling merciless, precise, tightening her grasp on the knife, leaving marks on the cutting board. It is seeing the best minds of her generation submit to the fantasy of security and mediocrity. How they all apparently accept having their cake but not eating it.

Sylvia cleaves another fennel bulb like a heart. She suspects that the others have had these thoughts too. They must have had doubts, known they'd dreamt of feeling something more, of falling more deeply in love. But the fear of loneliness outweighs those doubts. So instead of breaking up, getting divorced, they tell themselves, each other: well, maybe we're not in love anymore but we're a good team, good partners.

Are they cowards? Are they realists?

Yes.

She looks out the kitchen window, at the lake; by the edge of the woods Quince and Charlie are talking, making flower crowns, a boyish midsummer idyll.

She hesitates. Is she any better? Sylvia feels Charlie's expectancy, her patience, like a vacuum: I'm ready when you are. To have kids, to get married. Charlie already knows what breed of dog she wants, for when they eventually buy a house. The suction feels like love, it feels like gentle tyranny. Make yourself fit, sink into the frame. Or give it up and live alone. She doesn't want either.

But what does she want?

Esben, of course. She knows how great they would be together; there's always been something special between them, that he can't let her be, that she can't stop thinking about him. If they were a couple, if they lived together, it would never be boring – they would hold each other to an impressive standard. They would think and write and discuss together, and she would have an outlet for the unused intelligence, the excessive thoughts that are always accumulating – she would live up to her potential. With his gentle, thorough thought-fulness, he would help to get her thoughts in order, would see a light in her; she would be the best version of herself.

He is so good, so ethical, he would never be unfaith-ful to Karen, but could she say something? Would she be able to make him understand? That he could choose that future too. Choose her.

Of course, she doesn't want to ruin anything.

But she will ruin something, if there aren't any other options.

She isn't jealous, she realises, of Karen sleeping with Esben. She just doesn't understand why it has to be only Karen.

She turns back to Quince and Charlie, thinks how close they've become, unaware that they represent two needs in her. Freedom and safety. Could it be possible to have both? The lake is peaceful behind them, the scenery is so beautiful. And she thinks that this beauty is the key. This is where it can happen. This is where something new can emerge, something completely different.

Why not live here forever – maybe more people too – at the edge of the woods, in cabins along a lake? We could go around wearing kaftans (no, maybe that's too cultish? Perhaps optional summer attire instead; though she would look good in a tunic, wide and embroidered, bare tanned feet), eating pasta shells and figs, grilled mushrooms, anchovies and apricots, pomegranate desserts at their communal dinners; ripe tomatoes, saffron; totally Sapphic, pansexual (she looks tenderly at the fennel bulb, now diced, just imagine eating you at a utopian feast). We could live in this clear air, and we'd all sleep soundly, not just the kids, though we could take care of each other's kids. We could wake up early and well rested and kiss at dawn, read aloud to each other, constitute each other's problems.

How would we make a living? her inner realist asks (a weak voice). Sylvia shoos the thought away. Most of them already make a living writing: at the university, for newspapers, books. They could easily do that from here – there's internet in the woods after all. They could write together (she's getting excited now), read each other's writing and critique it, study theory, like they used to in the library, but for real. They could help each other choose the right words, to develop analyses, real intellectual activity, not her usual obstinacy. Would people refer to them deferentially, as a School? Her vanity swells. They would discuss the state of the world over dinner, and finally she would be tuned into current events (Karen, Adam would explain them to her, talk socio-economic sense into her), and Esben would teach the children to read Rilke. It would all cross-pollinate, poetry and politics, the extravagant platters of vegetarian fare – she would eat whatever was served; Gry would teach her to transform dinosaur kale and legumes into delicacies, she would become active like Karen, strong like the kids, jumping in the water with their healthy tanned bodies, climbing the trees (she stops herself – is there something a little bit fascist about the ripped children?).

It wouldn't have to be a commune, a Bullerby kibbutz. That would be too clichéd; there's something sad and unsettling about white people trying to live like indigenous people, self-sufficient and sustainable, like everyone who's moved to the Danish islands, Møn and Southern Funen, to stay home with the kids and card wool, their own holier-than-thou cults. It would have to be less ascetic, sexier, something achievable.

They could stay in the city, in their apartments. Maybe they could live in the same building – they could put those giant modular sofas to use and spend more nights together, lounge about, intertwined? Reawaken that undergraduate life they've long since abandoned: debating, flirting, flushed fighting on a red-wine-soaked evening: What are we really talking about?

It is an acknowledged truth that they don't see each other more often because of work and kids. But it's also an excuse, work, the kids, to finally be as boring as they've been all along. To let go of that need to be interesting. Falling into a calm has-been existence, ruled by the joy and dread of routine. She needs to get out of this kitchen, see the others. She needs to talk to Quince. Her last hope, her last ally.

If Quince meets a cute guy or a cute girl or a cute person and has kids, Sylvia will commit hara-kiri. Or move in with them uninvited, become a bitter mad aunt, drunk before dinner every day, completely melodramatic and German about it, though in that case she'd at least learn to play the piano. Or the harmonica. Right when the kids are being put to bed.

*

Gry finishes chopping the vegetables that Sylvia abandoned, arranges the salad.

'How inconsiderate of her to leave like that,' Karen comments.

'It's fine,' Gry says. 'We're almost done.'

She doesn't know why she feels the need to smooth things out. Why can Karen just call something good and something bad behaviour, while she needs to sand down all the friction, make everyone happy, make sure nothing happens? Karen isn't afraid of anything.

When Gry first met Karen, she thought that she looked like a popular girl from school: tall, skinny and blonde, the first pick of friends. Gry had been a good student, playing cards during break time, writing in friendship books, a pony girl without a pony, and later, the one holding her drunk classmates' hair back. She had warmed herself with the humble feeling of superiority, the reassuring moral lesson from a thousand films: that popular girls were superficial, empty, that there was something malicious about the cheerleader archetype that wouldn't hold in the long run. That her time would come.

But then you grow up and meet Karen: prom queen 2.0, a new mutation, just as classically beautiful as the girls from school but a better feminist than you are, a citizen of the world, fearless, gifted, fluent in geopolitics. And then you've got no choice but to become friends, because how could you even compete?

But there's no reason to feel inferior, Gry reminds herself. She wants Karen to see her as more than just her best friend and a good mum. She is intelligent too – she can talk to Karen about serious things, about her research. Something academic. She glances out at the lake.

'You know, I've read about this lake. There are several myths. About mystical lights at night, the sound of oars in the water, as if boats were sailing over it.'

'I've never seen that,' Karen says, as if she's not really listening.

'No, of course, not in real life,' Gry laughs. 'But it's classic folklore,' she explains, 'there are often local figures bound to lakes, archetypes like the Nøkken or the meadow elves, who are devilish but also erotic, even playful. Ready to lure you to your doom. This is actually what I'm working on right now. I've been looking at old texts, studying how these figures come into being over time, how they give people licence to debauchery. To explain why people do things they wouldn't otherwise. But you grew up here. Have you heard any stories about the lake?'

'Not really.' Karen hesitates. She doesn't tell Gry the story of the ruined manor, or maybe castle, at the bottom of the lake. That you can see the glint of the bricks on a sunny day. Her parents told her the story when she was little. Everyone from the area knows it. That the peninsula they're on right now used to be an isthmus jutting out into the water, and in the Middle Ages there used to be a manor or a castle there called Freggelund. One night some of the maids were drunk and tucked a slaughtered pig into a bed. They sent for the priest to give the last rites. But when he pulled back the sheets and saw the pig, he was so appalled by their disgraceful behaviour he cursed the entire place and as a punishment from God it sank down to the bottom of the lake, drowning the maids with it.

Karen washes the dishes; she doesn't tell Gry about the virgins from Freggelund, the maids who still haunt the forest, lovely women dressed in black that lure wanderers off the path, even though she knows it's exactly the kind of folk tale Gry is searching for. When she was little, she went looking for maids, walking fearlessly through the woods at night. Sometimes she imagined that she saw something: a thin, white mist hanging in the trees, but the virgins never came. Karen was furious. Was it because she wasn't a man?

Karen doesn't want her childhood memories to become part of Gry's research, its mix of magic and science, fairy tales and anthropology. It strikes her as unmethodical. It reminds her of how so many otherwise respectable women have started identifying as witches, making astrological charts, a slapdash concoction of self-help, spirituality and easy feminism. The steady stream of them flowing from the humanities into society, writing soft, theoretical essays about radical care or the metaphor of weaving, or how to be more like a seed. Holding hands and dyeing wool in bog water, thinking that they're radical leftists, even though their so-called ecocritical practice seems indifferentiable from being a stay-at-home mum. She is exasperated by her female friends, the conversations revolving around their private lives, social microdynamics and ascendants – how can so many gifted women waste their intelligence analysing their relationships or the phases of the moon. Whenever she hears the word 'retrograde', she imagines a city in Russia, can't help clearing her throat, turning the conversation to the war in Ukraine. Now she's here with her old friend, who she has missed, but it bothers her that Gry is intellectualising the woods instead of just being here – has she even gone swimming yet?

Karen grew up here; nature isn't metaphorical for her. The woods are the woods. Moreover. A part of her, deep down, does believe in the castle at the bottom of the lake.

Karen struggles to keep a straight face whenever Gry talks about her research, fights the impulse to laugh whenever she hears about the latest conference Gry has been to: Affective Archaeology or whatever. She's not laughing at Gry, she tells herself; she's laughing at the humanities. Karen was so relieved to finish her degree, to enter the real world. To be an intern, sitting in on editorial meetings and discussing current affairs. She had been warned about the media industry, the middle-aged men that still dominated it, but she clicked with them right away. They were direct, it was easy – she became their colleague and now they work for her, no problem at all.

Of course, she loves literature. She's marrying a writer. But all the theory, all the posturing, the eating disorders and pretty girls slogging away for free, infatuated by some narcissist poet just because he studied at the Creative Writing Academy.

She notices Gry, the natural movements of her hands, the visible veins as she runs a cloth over the counter. Gry, who has been such a faithful heart in their group, which would have fallen apart long ago if not for her. There is a warmth in her that Karen is thankful for, that she wouldn't know how to replicate, a pleasant thaw.

*

Quince and Charlie are sitting on the grass outside by the woods; they've started tying flowers into crowns, an unspoken aesthetic contest: flowering rush and blue-bells, tufted vetch, yarrow. Each in their rolled-up shirt sleeves; like two dashing boarding-school boys, Quince thinks contentedly. He tries to ignore the sight of the parked cars, ruining the pastoral landscape.

'I would never get a Tesla,' Charlie says.

Quince is smug: 'Typical Adam, why does he always have to be so dreadful?'

'I just meant that I would rather have an electric Volvo. In sage green. What's wrong with Adam?'

Quince makes a face.

'He's just direct,' Charlie says. 'It's easy to relax around him. Sometimes as a group you can be a little . . .'

'I think he's tiresome. Always a bit churlish. He doesn't seem to care whether or not you like him.'

'Maybe he just knows who he is?'

That Charlie doesn't share Quince's irritation only makes it grow. He sneers as he twists flower stems around each other.

'He just struts around all tall and handsome and brusque, arrogant in that intriguing way. Okay, Mr Darcy, *groundbreaking*. He's the kind of guy who would never see a therapist because he "thinks people talk too much about their feelings", but *if* he did, it would be all: daddy, daddy, daddy.'

He picks up an aster, he's worked up now.

'We've all known that popular boy at school, who

played football and guitar and had the wind at his back. He's so predictable and so boring. He studies some kind of social science, gets married, has some overpaid job. Life never deals him any blows; he has never thought twice about his private life. And still everyone is impressed, even though of course you know who you are if that's how you've grown up. Seriously, is there anything more boring than a person without a single complex? Everyone likes Adam, but in the same way everyone likes . . . vanilla, it's nothing special. You know what the bard Shania Twain would say about whether or not that would impress me.'

Quince could keep going with several more pointed comments, but Charlie has no patience for shit talking.

'Maybe you should look inwards. Why does Adam bother you so much?' she suggests. Quince looks up at her, pissed off.

'Because he is the way that he is.'

Charlie waits. As if she is expecting more from Quince. He takes a deep breath.

'Okay, fine. Maybe it's not him personally. But he just reminds me of how men have been for centuries, the whole old-world order. I have trouble with men who exist in the world like jellyfish in water. Like they're made of the same stuff as society. They're congruent. So, they can just blob around having a good old time without realising how easy things are for them.'

He feels his breathing quicken. He's not trying to be funny now, he's following his thoughts:

'And all the while I'm here . . . like an extravaganza. And I like that! But. I do feel weird when I'm confronted with these models that still have their factory settings intact. Who can inhabit the world and feel at home in it, self-reliant, who don't have anything to prove. Maybe I'd like to be like that too. Isn't it strange that people like him exist, who don't see themselves from the outside, who are never nervous in group settings?'

'I don't get nervous in groups,' Charlie says.

'Yeah yeah! Of course you do.'

Charlie smiles without looking up.

'Okay, but we're not talking about me.'

'Fine, then let's talk more about me then. I've spent the last however many years moving towards something masculine, yearning to feel at home there. And when I see Adam's brand of masculinity I think: Oh, what a dream! And: Oh, my old enemy!'

Quince sighs. Reflects.

'And it's not that I want, you know, to be some "classic man", but the ideal doesn't disappear, no matter how Pan and liberated I try to be. And I can feel this impulse to try to emulate that ideal, or exceed it, or to not care about it, or all those at once. But even if I want to "surpass" it, I still feel trapped by it, like a wilful child having a meltdown in front of his patriarchal dad. In which case you're not actually liberated, just contrarian. You still want affirmation, recognition, and that's embarrassing, which is why I would rather have as little to do with him as possible. I can't afford to admit there's something to that understated, assertive Tesla masculinity, because that would just be a bummer, because I have no natural proclivity for that. And I just know that he's looking at me, thinking, what a drama queen.'

Quince discards a daisy. Charlie smiles, speaks softly, kindly, as if Quince were a hyperventilating child. Quince acknowledges his defensiveness, paranoia – he hadn't realised there were so many hidden facets to his antipathy.

'Maybe you should give that part of you a chance,' Charlie suggests. 'Without worrying too much about it? Maybe this is about you wanting to feel more secure with who you are, and the problem is that something about that is bound up with classic manhood, which you've learned to be suspicious of.'

Charlie leans back.

Quince looks down at his woven flowers.

Could he just be natural?

As if.

'And you could just not care about what he thinks,' Charlie adds.

Quince snorts.

'Obviously, I hate that I'm even thinking about him in the first place. But it's difficult to be indifferent. I'm not the only one. It's so triggering to see everyone eating it up, the aura of these tall, authoritative men. Even though we like to think we've moved beyond that masculine stereotype, we all still take this guilty pleasure in it. You should have seen Sylvia before, when

Adam told her: "That book you're reading is shit." She loved it, she just wanted to be put in her place.'

Charlie is quiet.

'I think we're still pining for that angry-dad energy that we claim to be over. We've spent so many years getting over that kind of guy, becoming good, critical feminists. And still, all it takes is one strong, brusque man to make us forget it all. Why is that? Maybe it has to do with their arrogance, condescension, how they talk down to people, which affirms some shared inner inferiority complex. And we all want to change the perception that other people have of us, to please them or show them. Because maybe that will make the insecurity disappear, then we'll be okay. And it is easier to seek external affirmation – from a classic, recognisable figure of authority – than to affirm yourself, to assert your own self-worth.'

He feels relieved to have talked his way somewhere, dismantled the threat.

But Charlie seems uneasy. Distracted.

'Are you okay?'

'Sometimes I get insecure around people who are conventionally masculine too,' Charlie says softly. 'Even though it might be on a different level for me. Sometimes I feel like I have to measure up to a certain . . . well, confidence . . . with Sylvia, always be strong and still caring . . . do it all. Maybe I'm being too possessive or paranoid, but when your girlfriend is bisexual, sometimes I feel that I have to be better than all the women and better than all the men at once, or else she'll get bored.'

Oh, it must have been what he said about Sylvia and Adam and the book. Quince forgets how jealous Charlie can be. He's about to say that gender doesn't work like that, that she shouldn't feel the need to compete differently with men and women, that she shouldn't be suspicious of bisexuals.

Instead, he puts a hand on hers.

'I understand. But you have nothing to worry about.'

He wants to explain, tell her that she's a perfect human, that she is all of the good things men can be: protective, calm, steady, fucking like a world champion with something to prove, and none of the bad. Actually, flirting would be a good deed, he decides. Maybe it will repair something. He smiles languidly:

'Just to get it out in the open: Sylvia is ten times more attracted to you, and so am I for that matter. You have ten times more daddy energy, you can relax.'

Charlie looks down at her flowers, shy, but Quince hasn't gone too far. He has a sense for this kind of thing, it's a benign form of flattery. He leans back. Charlie is so reliable. As a matter of principle she doesn't flirt back, but she reaches over, pinches Quince's cheek, a little too long, a little too hard, as if to say: You're cute. As if to say: Watch yourself. Just as she would have done with Sylvia, and Quince sighs in feigned indignation, genuine glee.

He can feel the blood rushing to the sore spot on his

cheek like a blush. It's enough. They don't need to do more. They continue weaving their crowns in silence. Sylvia comes out of the house, takes a picture of them on her phone – does she look frazzled or happy?

*

At dinner, they talk about weddings. Gry thinks about hers and Adam's, how dizzying the logistics were, but she loved it. How it all came together. She doesn't like to be the centre of attention, but there was so much to do that she just disappeared into that, became part of something bigger.

Gry had felt so proud of her friends. How they stood out among the guests. Sitting under a chestnut tree in the garden. Karen in her unapologetically white shirt-dress, oblivious to wedding etiquette; Adam's best man had attempted to educate her on the matter and she had torn into him. *How many of the men here are wearing white shirts?* They were spectacular friends by the end of the evening.

Was that one of the few times they had all been together in the past couple of years? No, Quince hadn't come; had cancelled at the last minute, decided to stay another week in Berlin, maybe two. It doesn't bother her. Neither then nor now. The breaks, the absences, don't matter. Isn't it lovely, she thinks, that so much time can pass without seeing each other, and still it feels like they've never been apart? It's a sign of true friendship, to be separated without it having any significance, that they can move along like parallel lines. They have to. She feels bubbly. They need more weddings, please, more occasions to see each other. Just imagine, if the others had kids too and they could all play together.

Gry turns to Sylvia with a smile.

'Do you think you two will get married at some point?'

Sylvia feels Charlie's eyes on her, tries to keep her calm, as if Gry hasn't just tossed her a grenade.

'Maybe eventually,' she answers, and puts on her sunglasses. Hurries to pass the grenade on.

'What about you, Quince? Will *you* ever get married?'

Quince blinks, startled.

'Not anytime soon.'

Sylvia looks at him. Would she like to live like Quince, from one one-night stand to the next? Let herself experiment, follow her desire? Quince and his chronic Peter Pan syndrome; he doesn't ask for comfort or responsibility but only to enchant and be enchanted. And not see each other the next morning.

Adam leans back:

'Maybe not too long. I give it two years until you're in a committed relationship, moving in together. Everyone settles down eventually,' he says, sounding as convincing as a statistic. 'And then it's time to delete Grindr and get ready for the parents' WhatsApp group.'

'Even a parents' thread can be a dating app, if you're not a coward,' Quince quips. 'Weren't you just saying

we should be more like Bogart . . .' He deepens his voice
'. . . and *just do something*, just try something out, do
something crazy with your freedom?'

'I was talking about books, not saying that you
should go out and do it in reality,' Adam says.

Quince ignores him and turns to the rest of the
group, aware of his status as the only one not part of a
couple.

'I mean, I'm not judging any of you,' he assures them,
parodically tolerant. 'I just think you're all so *demonstra-
tive* about your *lifestyle* and *sexuality*. And I couldn't do
it, commit to this heteronormative, monogamous cult
of the nuclear family. But congrats on the wedding!'

They laugh, and Quince leans into his role as the
jester, the freedom to say whatever he feels.

'What *is* your sexual orientation anyway, Quince?'
Karen asks. (Gry winces; you can't just ask someone
that directly; or can you?)

'I think I represent . . . sexual disorientation,' he
answers, winking at Karen. She laughs.

'How long have you been sitting on that one?'

'Way too long.'

Sylvia clears her throat.

'Haven't we all become a little boring? Our lives are
so . . . homogenous. And solitary. What if we were more
communal? If we did something different? Could we
be – well, yeah, more disoriented? I just think back to
when we were at university. We used to see each other
all the time. And I thought our lives would be more

literary, more fantastical, that we would have figured out some brilliant, alternative way to live, our own way . . . something new.'

'Is that what you want? To start some commune out in the country with an orgy room, like they did back in the sixties? Because that worked out so well for everyone, just ask the kids,' Adam says.

'No.' Sylvia makes a face. (Does she?) 'I don't know what I want. But I do think I want . . . more. Don't you ever feel that way?'

Esben smiles, unruffled, like he hasn't heard her. He responds to Quince.

'I've also thought, why have a wedding? It's so old-fashioned. But at the same time, why pass up an opportunity to celebrate love? Love is precisely *not* that square life of the full-time job and nuclear family that none of us actually wants. That kind of life doesn't leave room for much besides itself. We hope the wedding will be a celebration of love, not just of me and Karen, but of all of us, because you are the most important people in our lives – you're all who we want to spend our lives with. Love should be all-encompassing.'

Sylvia stares at the table.

Esben reaches for her hand.

'It doesn't have to be so bleak.'

Quince rolls his eyes, placated; good enough. A summer wedding is irresistible, after all. They can go all out, throw a party for the ages.

Day 4

Sylvia walks into the sun, unfolds a blanket and lies down. She swallows. They are one day closer to the wedding, and she still doesn't know what to do. She feels an anger that isn't only about herself, about feeling rejected. It's bigger than that. Now they are finally here, and she had been looking forward to having time for each other, taking off, staying up late together, being a friendship group again. But it turns out that it's all about a wedding, a celebration of coupledom. She feels like she's been duped.

Esben is sitting under the umbrella, writing. His vows? Place cards? A toast? Sylvia desperately wants to know what is on the paper in front of him, and she really doesn't want to know.

He shouldn't be wasting his writing energy on something so superficial.

She remembers sneaking glances at him while he was writing on his legal pad in the library, always deep in concentration. They were so ugly, those pads; he didn't use leather-bound notebooks like the rest of them. He bought legal pads in packs of twenty-five because he filled them so quickly. He has always been so disciplined, modest; what mattered was the content.

Sylvia feels full of potential when they talk, when he nods thoughtfully at something she has said. When he listens to her, she has the sense of being recorded, that she is hearing her own voice more clearly. She loves that she still gets slightly nervous when they talk, an exposed feeling, like taking an exam. If they were a couple, that would be her normal state, then she would have the energy to finish boring books, she would understand that they weren't boring at all, she would rise up. That's how she sees him. As if he is standing on a higher plane, on a pedestal. Waiting to lift her up to his level. In real life, he has stage fright, but in her mind, he is always in the spotlight.

Sylvia remembers one summer when Esben was reading from his first book, the one about the saints that everyone praised, at an event on Møllegade. It was a political event, like everything was political when they were younger, to save the Amager Commons or for more public housing; she can't remember what they were fighting for that day, but she can remember Esben swaying on the stage, reticent but lucid. It was a dry summer, but honeydew dripped from the linden trees onto her bare arms. Meanwhile Esben was reading and looking like a young priestly prince, enveloped by his saintly tales, serious. The red blotches on his neck. It was quiet. The whole audience was in love with him.

But when did it start for her? The chaste but

charged night they spent together in his monkish bedroom? Earlier? As soon as she got to know him, she had a clear sense that there was an omniscience behind his quietness. She felt the opposite: that she always spoke to mask her ignorance. She longed to match his measured reserve.

Sylvia remembers Esben telling her once, in between lectures, about a writer he was reading, Pentti Saarikoski. They were sitting in the dry grass and the sun; Esben had been slightly febrile, as he was whenever he was taken by something, and Sylvia listened without really understanding what was so exciting. He was reading the novel for a book club, hosted by a little independent, idealistic publishing house. Sylvia had spiralled: should she read it too, this secret, essential Finnish masterpiece? Should she join a book club? Sylvia hadn't learned anything about the literary world from her parents, from school; she grew up in a small town, a middle-class home; her greatest shame: her stable, unimaginative upbringing; shelves of crime novels. She was left to discover real literature on her own: she borrowed Murakami from the public library, Jonas Gardell, Lotte Inuk, Michael Strunge and J. D. Salinger; she read haphazardly, falling for everything ill-adjusted, unaware of what was avant-garde, what was kitsch or mainstream, thinking everything was so sophisticated. But when she started at university, a whole new curriculum revealed itself, a whole sociology. It turned out that nothing she had read had been of real significance. She was constantly discovering new academic journals, new small bookshops, and whenever she flipped through this or that anthology, there was almost always something by Esben, wait, her friend? Already then: that sense that he was outpacing her, that he was an organic part of a world they now referred to in the definitive: *the* literary scene.

She studies Esben in the present. He is older, a new furrow by his mouth, but he still resembles himself, deep in thought, and then he looks up; a cheerful wave when their eyes meet. A little of his seriousness lifts when she is there.

*

Gry drops a handful of elderflowers into a wicker basket. She found it in the house; timeless, the woven lid, exactly like the one Jane Birkin had hanging on her arm in Paris in the 1960s, in all the photographs. For Gry, the wicker basket is more iconic than the Birkin bag. She walks over to the forest church to fill the basket with elderflowers, so they can make a cordial, more fried snacks. They're best harvested now, when they're in full bloom, wafting in the heat, before they wilt. A practical task. She loves it: the overflowing basket on her arm; maybe she'll take off her straw hat too, fill it to the brim, returning to the others like a fertility goddess.

She is in no rush.

She is rarely alone like this. Around her everything is quiet, buzzing. She wants to make an elderflower cordial for her friends, what kind of need is that anyway? It's like she has become even more generous from being here, in the woods; she recognises the desire to buy a round from the old days, but with the capacity of the present.

She likes taking care of people. She loves having guests, hosting, and waving off compliments. When the doorbell rings, she instinctively bends over, throwing her head to her knees, mussing her hair to make it even more voluminous. Rolls up her sleeves. Steps into the picture. She likes to epitomise generosity, to be energetic without being hasty. To arrange a dinner party, to be the one with abundance flowing from her. It comes naturally to her.

Of course, she's read theories of hidden reproductive labour, how women work more in the home, unpaid and invisible. But why can't you be a woman with a basket on one arm and a book under the other? Why do you have to choose a side, the intellectual life or the domestic one? She can work the whole first part of the day, she can cook, take care of the home, untangle children's hair, call a friend in the second part of the day – isn't that the work–life balance that everyone dreams of? She shakes the basket so that the flowers sink a little, making room for more; she doesn't feel like a victim.

On the contrary. Is there not a hint of egoism in the work of care, in motherliness? Giving and giving so that people are indebted to her, making all the desserts, remembering all the birthdays. Was it Marguerite

Duras who wrote about the mother's mild tyranny, her indirect control of everyone around her, she who has no power, shackling the members of the family to the home because they are indebted to her, all the love she has given them, all the comfort, the pillows she has fluffed, the rhubarb trifle; all that together creates a sigh, a gravity, that no one can resist without being ungrateful. In the end you run away from her screaming.

Gry picks another bunch of elderflowers. No, that's not how she is. Honestly, she's not demonic; she isn't French and omnipresent; she gives her children space.

She is an excellent mother; she can say that to herself, here, alone.

When she had Vera, without even thinking about it, she discovered a way to rock her when she needed to be soothed, a hand on the back of her head, a rhythm, a swaying in the body that was waiting inside her like old knowledge, a relief, she kept to herself. All of her friends were ready to be admitted with postnatal depression, they were reading critical books about motherhood, 'breaking the taboo', and saying aloud how terrible the early years were, and in secret Gry was loving it, the oxytocin taps were open wide, and Sejr followed, and she wants to have another one, maybe they'll have to buy an even more monstrous car, all the car seats for the kids. She feels it like a deep confidence inside her, she wants to be able to manage all the children there could be and not just manage but give them a wonderful life.

The birds sing above her.

But who is she? Is she a Moominmamma, creating a safe home and nurturing everyone, never herself needing to go out on strenuous adventures, risking anything, wanting anything, because she's too busy making jam, knitting sweaters, buying Christmas presents ahead of time? Convenient: never in danger, always ready to lend a hand, spreading out a tablecloth.

She has always made an effort to help, it comes naturally to her. She is mild, she doesn't need to draw attention to herself, she *gives*. But it was also a way to secure her residency in the friendship group, to compensate; is she still the one baking cupcakes for the reading group, nervous that she didn't understand the theory? What if the others never really liked her, only tolerated her? Do they find her boring? Banal?

Is there room for herself in her life? When isn't she thinking about fulfilling others' needs? She tells herself that work, the kids, family have taken up most of her private life, but honestly: Has she ever been a main character in her own life?

But can't the adventure also be an open home? That there is room for a whole flock of friends at their place, they just need to get through these early years, then they'll see each other again. Isn't it enough that her designer table is inclusive, that her friends are phenomenal, that they are edgy, difficult? She can make room for them, she can hold space for them, take care of them, she can adjust the smart lights that Adam has installed, as if they were gas lamps, make the atmosphere warm and intimate, cosy; she pictures herself with a ladle, pouring bowls of soup for them, creating coherence, and they hardly know that they are in it, that it washes over them, they just know that they are relaxed, that they can ask for another helping, another drink.

If she doesn't create the coherence, no one else will, none of the others think that way, about picking elder-flowers, they wouldn't get through a single day without her. If she only thought about herself.

But how would she spend her free time if she wasn't weaving a context for all of them?

She could try; she could say: It's your turn, friends. Delegate.

Ask Adam, *no*, tell Adam, to take the kids more often, that it shouldn't be her all the time. She wonders how he's doing; he's never spent this long with her friends before. She brushes the thought away. He's an adult, it's his responsibility, he can figure it out. Mostly, he talks to Karen, and suddenly he has tons to share about his work, funny stories to tell. It's so obvious, so touching, how much Karen resembles his mother, with her distance, her intellect; he tries to impress her like his frigid mother.

Did Adam choose Gry because she's the opposite, because she is warm, unintimidating? Does he take her seriously? They used to talk about the future all the time, he was interested in her perspectives, but something happens to the conversation when you've been together for a long time: the world becomes abbreviated, the frame of reference smaller, you talk about who's picking up the kids, about how obnoxious each other's friends are, thinking you know exactly what the other person will say.

The last couple of nights she has heard sounds through the walls, muffled orgasms. She was caught off guard, by how they continued, kept going, how many times in a row. It had got under her skin, like an itch, Adam fast asleep beside her.

The wicker basket is teeming.

She'd love for them to have sex soon. No. *Fuck* soon.

*

Quince flops onto Sylvia's blanket. Her eyes are closed; is she sleeping or just lost in thought? Esben is writing, probably working on one of his boring books. Quince has tried to read them, but he finds them so dry. He suspects the others are just being polite, pretending Esben's writing speaks to them.

Now Adam is on the way over too. He stops by the umbrella, looks over Esben's shoulders with his arms crossed, unabashedly reads along. He isn't unfriendly, just frankly states:

'Your handwriting is atrocious.'

'Okay?'

Esben sounds more intrigued than insulted.

Quince watches from a distance. Adam is so rude, and yet it is exciting when he continues, droning, he takes his time with the jokey insults.

'You write like Sejr talks. Even Gry and I can barely understand what he's saying.'

A hand on Esben's shoulder, exaggeratedly paternal.

'Get your shit together, yeah?'

His tone is direct, man-to-man, as if Adam has been summoned to testify, a casual accusation to assert the order of things. At the same time, it's just a wind-up, a cheeky comment, not a conflict to be escalated.

Quince moves over on the blanket, squints at the sun, relieved to realise that this is just Adam's disposition: small jabs for everyone, not out of hostility, but just because that's the way he is. Maybe we don't actually have an issue.

Esben lets himself be scolded, smiles up at Adam with narrowed eyes as if to ask: Are you done yet?

He is wearing a thin knitted vest, bare arms, large airy armholes, so you can see a little of his upper body; he does a lot with a little, Quince takes note, and it's typical Esben, underplayed. He is so reserved. He never makes himself known. Quince has always thought there was something stingy about that. Saving his thoughts, his charisma, for his books. As if it were more important to have something considered to say to the public than to those closest to you, and besides you never really feel that close to Esben.

All of them are so reverent around Esben, his seriousness, his books; so he becomes even more of a Hamlet, distant and princelike in his meticulously dosed madness, but Adam approaches him like he

would any of his friends, it doesn't have to be so difficult; it's probably a relief for them both.

Adam isn't done. He runs a hand over Esben's
triceps, plays impressed, winks.

'Have you been working out? Karen is a lucky
woman.'

Sylvia opens her eyes. She and Quince trade a glance,
knowing they just heard and saw the same thing. Simul-
taneously raised eyebrows, as if to ask: Why are they so
cringy? But also: How was that so dirty?

'I didn't know they were allowed to do that. Or that
they were capable,' Sylvia whispers, and Quince knows
what she means. It feels sensational for heterosexual
men to flirt with each other, ironically, but, never-
theless. Why not improve each other's handwriting,
comment on each other's muscles, in jest?

Just natural, masculine friendship.

What a privilege. Quince and Sylvia, have they ever
felt natural? They have made their personalities out of
being self-conscious, thinking twice about everything.

'I think they can, men nowadays. It's crazy what's
happened. My students, the guys, with their pearls
and earrings, they're so loving to each other, totally
gentle and open and caring. And a hundred per cent
straight. I don't get it, it makes me feel insanely old,
it's awful.'

'I get so mad thinking about being born a decade too
early,' Sylvia says. 'When we were younger the standard
setting was homophobia, and now it's pansexual

tolerance. I would get so much more out of my youth if I were young now, it's unfair.'

'You just have to decide to be ten years younger, like I do,' Quince says. But he knows what she means, that they both have a chronic nervousness saved up in their bodies. All while they're supposed to be at ease with who they are, be *proud*, a sassy best friend, a liberated bi person.

He could never figure out whether hetero girls, his peers, were flirting with him or just being nice, like all studious girls are practised in consideration. He was shy back then, but now he's having his revenge; he falls easily into conversation with people, into dancing, kissing, fucking. He decided once and for all: to be extravagant, generous with himself, and the world took note.

But oh, Sylvia. The two of them have always been perfectly platonic, through all his body's stages. They're both mannered, fictitious, but he knows paradoxically they make each other feel more real than anyone else. They are kittens together; she can nuzzle his neck, like now, and they know that it only means: You are my friend. You are my beloved friend. It would have been easy if they had been in love but they're like two batteries with the same end, there's no tension. It's a relief for them both, who otherwise experience the world as constant friction.

Quince looks up; now, heaven help him, Esben and Adam are kicking around a football, idly, nimbly, the most masculine gatekeeping practice, men's natural effortlessness with a ball. He's never played, God no. Not even as a kid, he was never a 'tomboy' in that sense. But Quince remembers once at university, one autumn, that Esben had started playing football, they all went to watch one of his games, cheer him on and ironise from the sidelines, through the drizzle, as the night fell, and the powerful lights turned the football pitch into a stage. An intricate ritual, the football match, Quince remembers, the cheeky uniforms, muddy knee socks, wet locks of hair clinging to their foreheads, short messages, shouting, but no one shouting, 'Sorry,' if they made a mistake. Efficient, coded, military communication: Man on! What did that mean? Man up? Quince remembers that Esben was new, in his tank top, not the team's real shirts, really trying, compensating, racing around, bright red in the twilight; how the excited body heat left him at half-time, in the drizzle, while the players caught their breath, huddled up to strategise. Esben must have seemed cold, because one of the other, more experienced players had silently unzipped his jacket and put it over Esben's shoulders, keeping his hands there as if to transfer the heat, a head taller. The memory glows in Quince; the natural care that lay in those hands, like an older brother; are you allowed to do that, are footballers allowed to do that? Is that also a task to be solved, a freezing teammate?

Was he jealous back then? Is he jealous now? Of what? Being a football boy? That cliché? Yes, but more specifically; of finding a way into a community where you take care of each other, where you can be an absolute beginner, and someone will paternally take you under their wing.

It has always been a tempting, terrifying, undiscovered land: how men behave in the company of other men. Are they more brutal, softer? He has dreamed about, he has had nightmares about, the locker room. The smell, the tone. For such a long time he has felt like a scientist who is desperate to observe quantum particles, but who disturbs their natural state with his presence; so it was too late to experience a pure, manly space and puncture it with his body. But what about now? Should he give in to something casual, learn to kick a ball, juggle, is that what it's called, ignore a lifetime of socialisation?

Sylvia interrupts his train of thought.

'But why do you think that *we* find it so exciting when they play at flirting?'

'Maybe it's just exotic and hot, like lesbians seen from a straight male gaze?'

Quince reflects.

'It must be the element of surprise. That they have a little more to them than you imagined. As queer people we probably underestimate heteros, see them as more inhibited and conservative and boring than they actually are. You become a little judgemental, a little sceptical from spending most of your life feeling different. So, we think: At least we have a patent on too-much-ness, on being scandalous. We are way more shocked by straight men touching each other's arms than they are.'

'Maybe there's also a feeling of grief or injustice because women and queers used to have an exclusive claim to affection, but now men are learning how to be more affectionate, which is wonderful, but then how are we supposed to feel superior?' Sylvia suggests, only half ironically.

Sylvia thinks: How fantastic that they are touching each other's arms, how liberated, if only it was a foreshadowing, of something opening, becoming fluid, everyone flirting with everyone.

Quince wonders: Could I make the same joke, join the circle? Would it feel good, would it feel like being one of the guys?

Sylvia thinks: Maybe everyone *is allowed to* flirt with everyone. But then again, it is just that: flirting, goofing around, writing in water; it doesn't really count.

She snorts away the dejection; they continue to gossip about Esben and Adam, with love, of course.

'They are so sure of themselves, with that solid hetero-masculine foundation. And paradoxically, that makes them supple, so they can permit themselves to do whatever.'

Quince nods. He exaggerates, yawns, his words strike a balance between awe and mockery:

'Straight men are one of the most flexible, unbiased sexual groups. They can stretch the limits; they could blow each other and it would still be in the name of friendship, wouldn't make them any less straight. Groups of these men are always entering, you know, *our* clubs, friendship groups, out on some kind of rampage after years of family life, and then they take some drugs like in the old days, then they go and look and feel unhampered and curious, and then one of them is brave, then one of them dances with some of the guys, and then there he is, making out to save his life.'

'And it probably wouldn't count as cheating,' Sylvia sighs.

They linger in their respective imaginations for a moment; football men in each other's arms; where would it happen, among friends, among the reeds, by the shore; how far would they go?

Quince is grateful that he and Sylvia can talk about everything, privately, in jest, but half sincerely. And then there is still something bitter there, as if their whispering confirms that they are tainted somehow. That they are a little on the outside. Too eager, too attentive, on the lookout, with a weak but cunning predator's gaze on the healthy, unworried sexuality that Adam and Esben are hardly aware of, that they carry around. He feels his age again. If they were young, they would have broken free of all these heteronormative complexes, Quince thinks.

'Are we sick?' he asks.

Sylvia responds reassuringly: 'No, we are *slightly* morally corrupt. A proud queer tradition. And that is something that all these poor, liberated younglings will miss out on.'

They sit there for a while.

'C'mere,' Sylvia says. She pulls Quince up. Waits until they are a safe distance from the house.

'There's something I need to tell you.'

'What's up?'

'I'm freaking out a little because . . . I love Charlie, but you know, it's hard. She's so perfect, but sometimes I feel so suffocated. And then I feel guilty for feeling suffocated.'

Quince takes her hand as they walk.

'I know that, honey,' he says supportively.

'Well, yeah. But what makes it grotesque . . . listen, you have to keep your mouth shut; you can't scream. It's just that . . . that I think I've always been in love with Esben.'

Quince throws his hands in front of his mouth, squeals behind them. He's shocked, exhilarated. Imagine this, a true scandal.

'There's always been something there, and I've been waiting for it to pass. But I've realised that I don't want it to. And now he's getting married. I don't know what to do.'

'Oh, my dear. I need to process this. Okay, poor you. But also: wow. Real, incredible wow.'

Sylvia exhales. Quince tries not to smile.

'Does Charlie know?'

'No.'

'Does Esben know?'

'No.'

'Am I the only one who knows?'

'Stop sounding so excited!'

'Sorry. It's just. Jeez. *My Best Friend's Wedding*!'

'Yeah, well. How about a little sympathy?'

'Argh, what are we going to do about this?'

'I don't know. What would you do? No offence, but you're a little more . . . you. Sorry, I don't mean to slut-shame you.'

'No worries, you're fine. Honestly, if anyone should be slut-shamed, it's everyone else for not being slutty enough. You can be an ethical slut. You could try to talk to them. Figure out what's possible?'

'That would be my nightmare. Saying it aloud. It never goes how I've imagined. You couldn't dream of how well I prepare. I craft these long internal dialogues, but when I'm there, talking to other people, they always say something totally different than what I expect, and then I can't find what I was trying to say in the first place. I wish it could just . . . happen. That he would kiss me.'

'Well, personally I think that one should be allowed to cheat in moderation. To misbehave a little. As we were just saying: our generation is so worried about being good. I think we owe it to each other to loosen up, a bit of hedonism, a bit of debauchery. And cheating isn't a crime, it's a . . . what's the word, a peccadillo. Not punishable.'

'Not according to Charlie,' Sylvia sighs.

Quince considers.

'But wouldn't it be even better if you went about it properly? If you talked to them, if it was open? Who knows, it's possible that Charlie will think it's totally fine, that Esben thinks it's totally fine, that Karen does too. You could make some kind of cute schedule. Take turns going out, take turns having multiple orgasms, take turns having kids, take turns taking care of the kids. You don't have to cheat in some kind of dramatic, destructive way; people have all kinds of wholesome poly relationships, you and Karen and Esben could be a throuple, and Charlie could fire up a whole flock of kids and have her electric Volvo, and you could have endless joint bank accounts.'

Sylvia brightens. Could it really be that simple?

They keep walking, silent. It's a relief just to say it aloud, to say it to Quince, to be herself. She can hear the birds. Everything feels right, honest. Her heart lifts. And yet there is still a knot in her stomach – because now it's real, now it's out there and now she has to do something about it.

*

Gry returns from the forest church with a basket full of elderflowers. The others are sitting around the table, drinking afternoon coffee, drinking water, their bodies turned lazily towards the sun. Quince has reluctantly put on his linen pyjamas, shorts and a shirt, so irradiated by the sun that his skin is starting to ache.

'Quince and Adam, could you take a run? There are a bunch of flowers I couldn't reach, and you're the tallest,' Gry says.

It's so childish, the pride that swells inside Quince, an honour as old as being picked out in the classroom; it's irresistible to be the one who can reach, the strong one.

'Shall we?' Adam stretches, and he's already up. Quince follows, trying not to think about how this is a world historical event: this *we* has never existed before. He decides to be friendly, neutral, not to say anything before Adam does, before there's a tone to modulate. They walk down the path into the forest together.

Karen watches them as they go.

She narrows her eyes.

Then she crosses her arms, addresses Gry.

'I'm just as tall as Quince.'

Quince and Adam reach the wooded church, the infinite thicket of elder, pick sprinkling, milky white blossoms in the heat, reaching up. It's not so bad, this quiet productivity. Quince tries it on like an outfit.

'We should also leave some, so it's not stripped bare for the ceremony,' Adam realises.

'Mm,' Quince affirms. How new and exciting, to be tight-lipped. How little can he say?

'But it's also fine,' Adam continues, 'if it's not too idyllic. To be honest, I'm kind of sick of summer weddings, having been to five thousand of them.'

He picks the flowers efficiently, haughty in his

measured way, as if he's above it all; he's talking more than Quince is.

'Throwing a love fest and inviting all your friends. It's so self-congratulatory, like going around wearing your own merchandise. I'd like to see a wedding go completely to hell. It's always sunny, everything is adorable, everyone wearing light linen.'

Quince clears his throat, gestures down along himself, ironically apologising for his clothing.

'Well, okay, but it's different when it's you, you're like something out of a Baz Luhrmann movie.'

Quince smiles. It hits the mark, feels nice.

And what does Adam look like? A propaganda poster for the superiority of the Aryan race, its natural, Germanic predatory instincts; how can a side parting look so brutal?

Quince says nothing, content to be quiet and relaxed; let Adam be the chatterbox.

Could it be this simple, could they just be friends, easy as that?

'Isn't it funny that he's straight, considering what his films are like? Baz Luhrmann?' Quince asks.

'Seriously?'

Quince pulls up a picture on his phone, Baz Luhrmann at a premiere, with his arm around his wife.

Adam peers at the screen.

'He looks like someone who just fucks whoever he feels like. They both do.'

Quince doesn't say anything. But he thinks: Ha,

men gossip too, talk about celebrities, it's sensational. He turns his back to Adam to pick more elderflowers. The pines of their pagan church loom darkly above them.

'There are tons up there, but I can't quite reach.'

Adam can't either, doesn't need to try.

'Try pulling the branch towards you.'

Quince grabs the ridged stem further in, pulls the whole branch down, so the elderflowers shower over them.

'Okay, I'll just use you . . .'

Adam puts a hand on his shoulder, they're both warm from the sun, he supports his weight on Quince, a leap, so he can reach, picks the umbels and lets them fall to the ground. And Quince doesn't try to feel it, the naturalness to it, how it feels like gaining access to something, the football pitch, the locker room, something he doubted he would ever reach; how Adam, without a second thought, has the mandate to offer his permission, and he knows perfectly well that he should be above rejoicing over this, and so what, if something in him longs to be recognised, something more than his own affirmation of his peacock masculinity, something an older brother can give, that warmth in the belly. He feels his knees wanting to buckle, collapse in relief, but c'mon now, everything else in him wants to stay upright, feeling strong and right in the sun.

*

Sylvia is ready to die from ambivalence, walking through the woods, pushing the buggy. Gry asked her and Esben to take Sejr for a walk, promised he would fall asleep, but he keeps waking up, trying to climb out and play in the trees, by the shore, even though it's dark and murky along the path. Sylvia wants to let him, but Esben keeps nudging him carefully back into the buggy. Eventually Sejr drifts off, ridiculously peaceful under the pretty cream duvet and the flickering beech trees around them.

From the outside they look like a couple, if there was anyone in the woods to see them; from the outside they look like everything that Sylvia has got herself worked up about. It smells like resin, it swells in her, how much she wants this, but not exactly this, she wants him, she wants the woods, but a baby? The responsibility? She catches a glimpse of Sejr, relaxed and defenceless, the warm cheeks, heavy eyelids, she feels a prick of bad conscience; it's easy to resent the buggy, a large and general monstrosity, but the child, the particular, downy human, is its own secret being. Every child will grow up with their own strengths and complexes, and rebel against their parents. Every nuclear family becomes its own chamber play, she reminds herself, literature's greatest dramas are made from these banal doll's houses.

Is this what Esben wants? With Karen? In general? The drama, the doll's house? Would she be good at it? Not being a harmonious mother, obviously, but at being a dramatic mother, an Ibsen mother, conflicted and melodramatic? She hasn't considered it before now.

'Don't get offended, but I was thinking about what you said about more conventional ways of life not leaving much space for other things.'

'Did I say that?'

'Yesterday, at dinner, you said . . . that none of us really loves the square life. Are you afraid that part of you would be closed off by that life? I can just feel that when I'm walking around with this buggy and my friends are getting married that I have this resistance, that I'm afraid to become lulled into some bourgeois life that I won't be able to escape.'

Sylvia puts it as gently as she can, so it seems like it spontaneously occurred to her, genuine curiosity, not as if she is asking with all her desire in the pot. His usual thoughtful pause, and then:

'It's not that I love the conventional life as such. It's just, like I said, as if it fills the days with itself, and then you must be really wilful to insist on anything else. It's difficult for me, the thought of children. I would love to have a child one day, but you know how I feel, how my mum was . . .'

Sylvia forgets to listen as the words land inside her, shining amulets: I have to be brave; I have to be stubborn. If she is, would he run away with her? Esben stops speaking when she doesn't respond.

While they're walking through the woods, she's struggling to find a polite way to articulate her anger and loneliness, while trying to steer the awkward city buggy over the beech roots, but then her indignation turns to sympathy. She shouldn't be insulted, but have empathy with her friends, with all the young families who are finding it challenging. Doesn't she hear her friends' exhaustion, the resignation they call realism? Reassuring each other that no one is happy all the time?

'A while ago I was drinking wine with Gry and I asked her: Well, are you happy? Are you in love? And she answered pragmatically, content, that maybe she and Adam are not in love, like they used to be, but they are a "really good team".' (Sylvia says it with big air quotes, letting go of the buggy; Esben instinctively reaches to grab the handle.) 'They're good at making things "function".' (Sylvia is trying to keep her hands still, trying not to grimace.) 'And when someone says that kind of thing, Esben, the only thing I see is an enormous snowsuit, swishing and swishing around in an enormous dryer.'

She doesn't have the energy for some nuanced response, to be made to feel dumb and immature; suddenly she doesn't want him anymore, all his tempered reflections, his convenient realism.

'All I can see is a monster, forever devouring, regurgitating, chewing and gorging,' Esben says.

'Is that from *The Sorrows of Young Werther*?'

Esben smiles at the forest floor. Sylvia loves him so much.

How can they understand everything the other says, and still live in two separate worlds?

Is it just because he and Karen got together so young, and never tried anything else?

A cloud draws over the sun. Esben looks like a Sturm und Drang poet himself. Is he caught in this life, in the calm and stability, because he has all the other difficulties inside him; does he need Karen, her strength, because she's a lighthouse, a reliable authority, a foundation to his world?

That thought fills Sylvia with a strange, reverent envy, Esben's proximity to true insanity. She fears that her own nettling mental health isn't great, but in a less interesting way. Moderate anxiety, depressive periods, minor explosions of imposter syndrome; crying attacks when she suddenly sees herself from the outside and even though she's alone in her apartment asks herself acerbically: Are you just making a scene to make yourself seem interesting? Yes, she is fragile, but what kind of humanities grad isn't? It isn't the real deal, true insanity, where you hear the trees and sparrows speaking to you; the kind of spring that Esben never asked to be born with, but which he has found a way to draw off, let trickle in a controlled way out into the world. He is madder than she is, *and* he is more controlled, it's unbearable. She corrects herself, it's old-fashioned to call it insanity, probably politically incorrect and stigmatising; anyway, it's a cliché, the romantic myth of the artist, the notion that the genius can channel an inspiration that is both divine and pathological. But Esben *is* divine.

Karen and Esben are both intellectual artsy types. They could be like the Bloomsbury Group, think in terms of free love. They're the kind of people who could make it work. They aren't like Adam and Gry, a poster couple for the beige nuclear family. Maybe they could live a different kind of life?

Esben is a writer, for Christ's sake. Doesn't that entail a freer life?

She decides on an oblique approach.

'Can I ask you about something else?'

'Of course.'

'How. When you write . . . how do you go about it? Does it just come pouring out, or do you treat it like an office job?'

He looks at her, kindly misunderstands her question:

'Are you writing something?'

She is nowhere near writing anything, now that he's asked. She has tried. There have been various projects, expensive notebooks, but what comes out is embarrassing, overwrought, coquettish, too much like herself. She isn't interested in doing things she isn't already good at.

And yet: would he like her more if she was working on something? If she were bold and ambitious?

'Yes. Or. I'm trying, but it's difficult. It's difficult to write something that you don't think is any good.'

An inhale, a little twitch under his eye.

'Hm. Maybe you can try thinking that it has to be

bad to start with. Even though it feels really embarrassing. Because we are vain.'

He looks at her knowingly, as if they're talking about some shared character flaw, continues:

'Maybe you can turn it around and see something intriguing about that embarrassment? Something vulnerable. That you have to reveal yourself in order to formulate something that is tentative and honest and out of your control. Do you think you could approach it that way? Or is that too out there?'

She nods; can he tell she's turning red? If only you knew.

She shakes it off; comforts herself by noticing how the speckled shadows fall over Esben, bringing out his prominent cheekbones, how the forest scenography is conspiring with her to make him dramatic, even though he doesn't want to be. He wants to be understated, but good luck with that, she thinks tenderly, you've been born with a drama I can only dream of.

She has always, now that she thinks about it, had a habit of falling in love with her friends (with her enemies sure enough too) from childhood; for a long time it wasn't a possibility, living in the countryside and falling in love with both her girlfriends and their older brothers, it was doomed, but the feelings sprouted everywhere; in secondary school it was easier, it was easier to be a teenager, to be in her twenties, the feeling was more pure, hormonal, a simple, excited horniness, that wanted to rub itself up against anything, and which everyone felt; moreover they were always drunk – at university, her longing became more disciplined, abstract, daydreaming about whoever, who could be the right one, who could open her up. But then she met Esben, and he *was* the right one, but nothing ever came of it, and then she met Charlie, who is so good and solid, who takes care of her, who satisfies all her body's needs, but what about her mind? She can't figure it out. The teenage horniness has bled into the daydreams of adult life and the worries: if you're too uninhibited, you learn to be more inhibited, to hide your desire, but that has its costs, all the hiding places start to glow erotically, and there are fires to put out and fires to warm yourself by every which way.

Sylvia looks at Esben's shoulders, his hair, his simple white vest, his bare arms (he doesn't dress like a stormy poet, she respects that, she thinks it's too bad/a missed opportunity), she looks at his hands, his cuticles red where he picks at them and tries not to pick at them, and she thinks at the same time: Read aloud to me all the time, and: Maybe you could choke me a little with those pink piano fingers?

Is that what she wants?

If she is honest with herself, she wouldn't even know where to start, if they were to sleep together. She has thought about him for so long that he has become a symbol of yearning; her infatuation isn't rusty but has begun to oxidise, turn abstract. She would be sleeping with a decade of accumulated sublimation; good luck with that . . .

*

They carry the benches over and set up the chairs, sweating. They jump in the water, dry off in the sun, jump back in. They plan the day: a small procession to the ceremony in the woods, then they'll return to the house together. It will be so lovely. In the afternoon they're drowsy, so Gry suggests a game of boules; they drink a beer while they play.

Adam and Charlie make an overqualified team, wipe the floor with the rest of them. It's laughable how markedly better they are, their aim, their bodily intelligence, they bask in it, toss slowly and surely, win one round after another. They can't help getting caught up in it, gloating:

'Try not to throw like someone who studied comparative literature.'

On the other team: Gry and Quince are fine with it, laughing at their useless throws, but Karen is getting more and more upset, fuming at them. She hates losing.

'You've got to be kidding me,' she grumbles as Gry misses yet another shot.

Quince gives her a probing look.

'Karen, dearest? Take my hand.'

She wrinkles her brow, furious that he thinks she needs to be calmed, consoled.

'Why?'

Quince grabs Gry's hand instead.

'Doesn't this feel . . . awkward?'

'Yes! I don't mean to be rude, but this feels totally wrong. Why is that?'

'Can't you two pay attention?'

'Just try it, Karen,' Gry says.

'Fine, okay,' Karen says, limply holding her hand out, as Charlie knocks another ball with a warm, dry thunk.

Quince takes Karen by the hand, with his hand on top of hers.

'How does that feel?'

'Bizarre, like you're twisting my hand off.'

He lets go of them, blows into his hands like a magic trick, takes both their hands again.

'How about now?'

'Yes! This feels nice! What did you do?' Gry asks.

'I just turned our hands the other way. I wanted to see whether you're a natural overhand or underhand.'

'Is it some kind of sports technique?' Karen asks.

'Nah, more like a simple top/bottom test.'

Gry looks perplexed.

'Um, a kind of . . . personality test. Everyone likes to lead or be led. You can see a relationship's dynamics by looking at how a couple holds hands. If you take a child's hand, you'll naturally turn the back of your hand forward, because you're the one leading the way.'

Gry tries, she grasps the air, as if she's leading Vera or Sejr by the hand; it's true. Quince lets go of their hands, and he continues:

'And most men hold their girlfriends' hands in the same way, but that's their issue. When you see two women or two men . . . or two people, who are beyond those kinds of dated categories . . . it's a quick way to read whether you're a little more dominating or soft. Try holding each other's hands.'

They obey, it's easy; Gry turns her palm forward, Karen the back of her hand.

'See, you're a harmonious match,' Quince says. 'It's no exact science, but it tells us something about how desperately you need to win a game, or whether you can lose without being a little baby.'

Karen snorts, but she seems content now.

'And which one are you?'

'I do it all,' Quince says with a wink, shrugging his shoulders. They resume the game. He doesn't care about losing, feels above it all.

*

Sylvia and Esben are back from their walk. They sit down to watch the game from a blanket. Watch Quince's demonstration. Esben holds his hand up to Sylvia's, fingers spread; she intertwines her fingers in his, his fingertips rest on her knuckles, his pink nails. She is familiar with Quince's theory – feels elated, ha! She and Esben have a completely egalitarian dynamic. The others are back to playing. Esben and Sylvia let go of each other's hands to clap, cheer. Settling in the sun.

Eventually they doze off. Sunbathing has turned into

a nap. Esben is asleep beside her, on his side, stubble to the cotton blanket's turquoise and magenta hibiscus flowers, and now she's lying here, tormented and lucky, his breathing is so heavy. Sylvia snuggles into him. This must be permissible, it's perfectly innocent, but she's also going crazy from being able to feel him. His skin, the peachy undertone she knows so well, precisely peach; sometimes she forgets to appreciate how marvellous it is, that transition between pink and orange, a golden blush.

She lets herself be rocked into sleep, she shuts her eyes against the light, but it's not bothersome, the sunshine on her eyelids, the peachy warmth, like the backseat of a car, leaning against the window, like falling asleep as a small child. Sleep softens something, the caution; she moves closer to him, finds a place against his sun-warmed skin. A jolt in his thin sports shorts, she can feel his penis wake, getting hard, through the fabric. She almost weeps through her drowsiness and the light, the peach-tinted dream, at the desire that is finally somewhere besides her own body, that something in him is raised; it feels like a miracle. It's really happening; a sigh in her dream.

Then: a wave of guilt, this isn't allowed, he's sleeping, she comes back to herself, rolls onto her stomach, pressing her forehead against the blanket.

She gets up, feeling sleepy. Milky and crackling. The others have gone swimming, gone inside, it's deserted out here. She lets herself quietly into the bedroom; the air, the bed is still cool here. It's strange for her to be here without Charlie, there's something helpless about her desire – how does one take care of oneself?

She lies on the bed. Sylvia licks her fingers, feels them against her lips, her tongue. She tries to masturbate while dutifully thinking about Charlie, about her hands, it usually works; it isn't working, she feels too guilty, a shame running with the cool through the room. She tries to pull the peachiness, the warmth, the redness, in here, thinking about Esben, if he were touching her, if they were lying in tall grass, if the birch trees were flickering, if it always had been her, if he looked at her hungrily; but now she can't decide, is he wearing an engagement ring or not, both scenarios feel like a crime, even though it's a fantasy. Her spit-wettened fingertips glide over her clit, but she can't let go, can't shake the feeling of failure, of being in the middle of a failed, autoerotic version of Tove Ditlevsen's poem, 'The Eternal Three'.

She feels the loneliness, the coolness; she's losing steam. So, she decides to surrender to the loneliness, eroticise it, instead of thinking about Esben, or Charlie. She gets up, leans against the wall. She thinks about herself. She is so tangled, torn up. What if she were true to that entanglement, if she was strong despite it? If she dared to be alone. Later, in ten years, twenty years, she would be free and happy, independent, determined and brave and deeply connected to life. Her hands keep weaving the story, it's not strenuous anymore, the images give way to each other: getting up in the morning to write, honest, uncompromising, she's enough, she bears her age, her chaos, with dignity, she's wet, it's building up in her body now, she buckles but keeps herself up, her abdominal muscles quivering, her breath filling her whole body. It's so abstract but so irresistible: arriving at a stage of life when all the guilt, the doubt that haunts her now has been dealt with. Middle-aged and self-possessed, just the idea of relief feels like leaving the ground. She's never tried to come like this before, standing up, it feels as if something inside her, in her belly, is shattering into gravel. She falls to her knees, seeing herself before her: older, serene, worthy.

She gets up, flops down on the bed. Strangely proud. It feels authentic to come with herself as the main character. But the fantasy reminds her of something, what? It dawns on her sleepily, it's silly, but she remembers watching television one afternoon in her childhood living room, that the sketch of the fantasy stems from an episode of *Beverly Hills 90210*.

Kelly Taylor is given an ultimatum, she must choose between Dylan McKay and Brandon Walsh, her two love interests. They've decided. The three characters meet on a quiet street, alone. Finally, after a few days of consideration, they stand there, squinting in the strong Californian sun, Brandon and Dylan facing Kelly, like a duel in a Western. Who will she choose? The miracle is that Kelly says, I choose me, turns and walks away. Even though she loves them both. That was the first time Sylvia felt respect for Kelly Taylor.

But what if, Sylvia wonders, Kelly Taylor had gone even further, had declared: I choose you both, I choose the three of us. Imagine if the mythological teenagers had been able to lean into each other, the sun making their outlines glimmer, imagine if Brandon and Dylan had been able to see each other's rolled-up sleeves, terrific hair and soft eyes and not seen a rival but an oasis, a place to rest their desire.

There's no end to the number of fictional and real love triangles that could be solved with a little flexibility.

And yet it never happens. She doesn't know how the Californian *Fata Morgana* is supposed to become a reality. She wants to choose herself, she also wants to choose everything, Esben, Charlie. To breathe freely, engagement rings, becoming a waterway split into tributaries, taking the division in her core seriously. She has always had an urge to rebel, for freedom, but never possessed any decisiveness, no sense of direction, instead: a surplus of paths.

Can't I just love them both; I can share – could they?

She starts to believe that decisiveness is a trap too, a fallacy, that one person, one choice, should be enough, be the right thing. She has never dared to pull herself together and leave Charlie. Instead she has waffled: she has never dared to tell Esben directly about her feelings, maybe that is what she has to do, say: I want the two of you, or else I just want me. Could one be that utopian, go in multiple directions at once?

The idea of living with Charlie is claustrophobic, but so is the thought of living with Esben, all his books and pensiveness. The thought of living with anyone is claustrophobic. Maybe she was made to live in a tower like a slutty Rapunzel, hair falling like an invitation to various princes and princesses. Esben is a realist novel and so is Charlie. Everyone else is a realist novel, and she's a fairy tale. Why should she have to accommodate their narrow expectations?

She hears an echo of common sense, a cynical superego:

You can't have it all.

She twists the sheets in her hands. Relaxes her fingers.

But bitch, I might.

She sleeps, she dreams.

*

Gry comes out with drinks; Adam is making dinner inside. White port, tonic; they don't deserve her, Quince thinks; his glass is already empty. Gry asks if he'd like a refill.

'Would I ever! Let me get it. Sit back, relax.' He's up, his hands heavy on her shoulders. He stands like that for a moment. Maintaining eye contact. Does she need anything? She shakes her head, smiles, sinks into her chair.

'Yeah, you do. Wait here.'

Gry puts her hand on his.

'Will you see if Adam needs a hand?'

Quince crouches down next to her, whispers: 'How exactly does one ask Adam if he needs help?'

'You just ask,' she smiles.

He wavers outside the kitchen, slightly effervescent in the head, a drink in the sun on an empty stomach, feeling happy and right. Maybe he doesn't need another round, but he'll make a drink for Gry. He's taken off his pyjama shirt, now that the sun isn't so strong. As he steps inside, the darkness overwhelms him. He hesitates on the threshold, hanging in the broad white doorway. Bits of conversations, the clinking of glasses floats through the window. Adam is standing by the stove, stirring something in a small pot. The kitchen is a disaster, there's a discarded pot in the sink. Adam pours something hot into a pan of egg yolks, focused on whisking. Splashes the stovetop. Reaches for another pot and pours butter into it, slowly, a thin stream, whisking faster. High flame. Quince stretches to see what's happening, bites the inside of his cheek, not laughing when the mixture separates, slowly and surely. Adam throws the pot into the sink.

The door hinge squeaks, and Quince hurries inside, holding the glasses up as an explanation, opens the fridge.

'Is dinner ready?' he asks, as he pours the port and immediately knows it was the wrong question.

'No, the food's not ready yet.'

Adam is calm, persistent but angry. Is anger the only emotion cis men allow themselves to feel? If Quince was angry, he would hide it. Should he work on that, learn to be openly irritable? Would that be liberating? Or would it just force everyone around him to pay more attention to him?

Cis-het men and their cooking complexes; c'mon, chill out already.

He exhales, enjoying the cold from the refrigerator on his face. He could also just relax and not overthink every situation, he tells himself. Not everything has to be about masculinity. Remember, he and Adam are friends. He grabs a lime, closes the refrigerator door.

Adam starts on a new batch, strains the whites from the yolks through his fingers, next to a small dish of clarified butter. This is a signal to leave him alone, but Quince ignores it. He wants to help, to come closer to the anger, run the risk of setting him off.

'Are you having difficulty with that?'

Adam runs his hand over his forehead, leaving a bit of egg in one of his eyebrows.

'I don't get it. I've made a million hollandaises.'

Quince stands next to him, tries to be friendly, direct: let's solve this problem. He adjusts the dial on the stove.

'Hm. Why don't you turn down the heat?'

He can't help himself.

'You know, you don't have to do everything on your own. If you hold the pan and pour the butter *and* whisk at the same time, you'll make a mess. You know, you can ask a friend for help.'

Adam doesn't respond.

Quince grabs the little pot of melted butter.

'Here, let me pour.'

Adam whisks: the sauce thickens. Quince puts a hand on Adam's shoulder; exaggeratedly arrogant, he instructs: 'If it separates, just add a few drops of cold water. And if you add a bit of whipped cream, you'll have a mousseline, which, you know, is even more sophisticated.'

Adam makes a face, doesn't say a word.

'By the way, you've got some egg in your eyebrow.'

Quince turns to leave and return to the others, feeling good. He pauses by the door.

'Wait, can I taste it? Is it the standard bay-leaf version?'

'Actually, I used a decent amount of vermouth.'

Adam dunks a teaspoon into the pot. Quince is still standing by the door, holding the glasses. Adam looks at him. Quince stays where he is – now he's just being annoying, testing to see who will give in first.

Adam approaches him.

And now I have to make a microdecision, Quince thinks. Should I take the spoon and taste it myself, or should I open my mouth? He lives for this kind of thing. How great is the distance between us; how intimate can I make this situation? Quince hesitates. He stays where he is, and opens his mouth expectantly. He wants to see if Adam will play along; so what, is it gay if you're friends? We are friends, right? After the elderflowers? Is he squandering their new bond? Oh well, too late now.

Adam puts the spoon in his mouth, an indifferent expression on his face.

A jolt goes through him. It was just a whim. But now something is opening up inside him. In his lower belly. Dark and quiet, but powerful, like a universe expanding.

He tries his best to look normal.

'It works,' he says, stepping backwards into the evening light.

Quince sets the glasses down in front of Gry, continues down to the lake, wades ankle-deep into the water. Dizzy. What the fuck. It was supposed to be a joke. But standing there, waiting, with his mouth open, with the spoon in his mouth. The moment has passed, but now everything inside him is begging: More! More!

For once they were both just being themselves.

What is this feeling? The quiver in his belly. As if something he didn't even know was locked up has been released.

He takes slow, conscious breaths, feeling his body betray him, getting wet, hard.

Again, his body whines: Go back.

Oh no, he whispers to the lake.

Not that.

Not him.

Day 5

The air is cool, the night still suspended in the trees. Karen has wrapped herself in layers of wool, thick socks; she's wearing Esben's rain boots, standing by the water.

It's so quiet here. Everyone is sleeping, the world holding its breath, and this small shoreline is hers, the small ripples lapping against the sand, a thin film of foggy water. A voice inside her begs that the others won't wake, that the morning can be hers for a little while more. This cobweb state is so rare, finally she has a morning to herself, and now she's here. She can think, she can be herself. Will she have forty-five minutes, three hours?

She woke up at 5 a.m., and it was already light, a milky morning light, the sun's first rays, already up at 4:22, as if to say: I'm waiting for you, everything is ready for you. Patient. The air is grey and light and mild. For once, it's cool, after these summer days one after the next, faithful, excessive. You sleep, exhausted by the sun, wake in the heat that has already gathered, the day is fully baked by 7 a.m., you don't have a chance.

She feels the cold, the dew, clearing her head.

If only every day could be a dewy June morning, spent alone.

What should she do with the morning? She could read. Write. Go for a swim. The water is probably warmer than the air right now.

She knows this is her strength. Being at ease with herself. Not needing to share the moment, the morning's bated breath, with anyone. Her discretion is a refined form of egoism, that she is capable of enjoying things in peace. As part of a generation that has a constant need to share, to be recognised. She feels her journalist voice revving up, hushes it, not now.

She knows that her sense of self-worth is on the edge of tipping over into cockiness; she maintains a close watch to make sure it doesn't.

The tall belts of Douglas firs are steaming on the opposite shore, dark blue in the morning; a bank of fatty, white fog rising from them and becoming one with the sky.

The cold isn't unpleasant, isn't the kind of chill that settles like a flu. She can feel her fingers contracting, slimmer; her engagement ring slides more easily over her knuckle. She feels pure, virginal in the dawn. But she isn't virginal, she thinks, drily; in fact, her period is late. She hasn't told anyone, she still doesn't know how a child would fit into their lives.

She doesn't want to not be at work.

She already misses the editorial team, the

discussions. She misses the world, the fresh crises. She left the woods, the lake and her family because she wanted to get out. Just five years ago, Esben followed her around the world while she was working as a foreign correspondent – they spent six months in Jerusalem, Brussels, Delhi. He was the one who wanted to return to Denmark, when they started talking about kids; he wanted to be closer to their parents, their friends, the Danish welfare system.

She misses her morning routines abroad, their chef in India. Esben hated it, how much their money was worth, that they had an *employee*.

And now she has to live in Copenhagen, because they might have a kid who will need to be in day care. Even if she and Esben split up, she will have to live in the same city, the same country, to share custody.

Or would she leave them?

She considers it, sees herself stepping onto a plane, Ingrid Bergman in *Casablanca*, but alone, an impressive, tragic gesture, she would relinquish them, the child and Esben, so that the child's world wouldn't have to be split. She would be a modern Medea, and in the sacrifice, there would lie a freedom, a departure:

> Let my children know,
> that their mother loved them,
> she just didn't have the energy

She dismisses the thought. Daydreams are nonsensical. She thinks about her work, something tangible. She needs to fire two journalists next week, she knows how to tackle it, she's looking forward to having it over with, she knows who she'll bring on instead. Should she feel worse about it? Is she too tough? Cold? Is there something wrong with her? Should she have more sympathy, what kind of a mother would she even be?

She's unsure when she sees Gry making motherhood look so easy; she's a natural force, warm, attentive, she clears the table, gets the children to taste grilled perch, turns it into a game. Gry has the knack for it, she reminds herself, and she has *time*. Gry doesn't work much. Does she even have a real job? Isn't she just killing time between graduate school and whatever's next? Going to conferences, advising students, researching aquatic plants. The embellished retellings: Karen recalls the time Gry was cat-sitting for a Swedish professor, called it a *residency*. Gry has the time to knit, bake sourdough bread, ferment things, recommend books about ecofiction and hydrofeminism they should read. Meanwhile, Adam makes enough money for them both, to decorate their apartment, tasteful and beige.

Karen straightens up. Esben's Danish Arts Foundation grants are a form of recognition, but they are purely symbolic in the grand scheme of their budget. She makes the money in their relationship. Esben can take the full year of parental leave, if need be.

She sighs.

She hopes that the others won't ever wake and puncture the bright majestic morning, which is hers alone. She imagines herself as a kind of guard post, as she ties her hair back into a bun, she doesn't want to be anyone's mother, but she has always felt that she would be a natural, old-fashioned kind of father. Her distanced paternalism, like how she prefers time away from them, her friends, but likes taking care of them from a distance. She is whole, independent; she knows that is exactly how Esben sees her too. Is that why he loves her, because she's strong, because she doesn't need anything from him?

With him, she never feels too tough, wrong.

Karen is grateful for that.

She sits down and admires the lake. She's known the sparkling water, the belts of trees on the horizon her whole life.

She has an idea. She'll walk over to the nearby stream, where she used to catch crayfish with her father as a child. There are traps in the shed, this is right when you're supposed to catch them, at dawn. How perfect, they can have a crayfish party tonight, they can catch more for the wedding. The crayfish are too small now – you're only allowed to take them later in the summer, but she doesn't care, they've already broken the rules, and in all honesty, this is her forest. She enjoys the image. Herself as a hunter, the others waking up to her fresh catch, that it doesn't have to be some group activity.

It should always be like this, a dewy June morning to yourself.

No, it has to be fleeting.

You have to savour the pockets you find, try to remember that this state will return, even if you forget the feeling of it: of purity, that liminal space between dreaming and waking, aware and alone, before the veil of the shared world is pulled aside, part of the world's preparations; to be here, quiet as a mouse, like a spectator at a dress rehearsal.

The clear, quiet morning, the fresh air, before the day is saturated with colours, heat, sounds, thousands of conversations, before all the love and idiocy, drama and banality that fills the human hours begins.

*

Sylvia and Quince are hanging fairy lights and chiffon scarves in the trees over the lounge chairs. Between them: a large platter of crayfish. Lemons. Crusty bread. It's late; Vera and Sejr are already asleep.

Sylvia is beside herself – maybe her dream can become a reality, if they just craft the right landscape, the mood that will make it all possible, so they can speak more openly and be free of their boundaries. Charlie, Adam, Gry, Esben and Karen can wade out to meet them.

Adam examines the decorations in the trees, arms crossed.

'You've made an effort.'

They all have. Karen is wearing a forest-green suit, hair pulled back tight. Esben is in an ochre shirt, embroidered, so long and loose it could almost be an indecisive dress. Would you call it a tunic? He looks like a young star from the Old Testament, maybe Joseph? So lovely in his tunic that his brothers became envious.

Quince is trying to look like he isn't making a big deal about it, white vest, cut-off jean shorts, everything is too short on him. Amethyst earrings: he wouldn't want to be too boring.

Gry is beautiful, draped in delicate cream knitwear, handmade and not very childproof. Quince gives her a hug, steps back, holds her shoulders as he looks her up and down.

'Good for you!'

'Thank you, but I don't know if it actually works,' she says.

'You're perfect.'

Quince takes out a pot of glitter face paint, dabs pink onto Gry's eyelids, up towards her eyebrows, a line over her collarbone. Carefully shakes her plaits to loosen them up a bit. Charlie has got in line behind Gry.

'Do you want some too?' Quince asks happily.

Quince studies Charlie's face. He dips his thumb into the glitter, spreads it slowly, ritualistically, over Charlie's forehead, makes his voice rumble: 'Simba.'

Charlie gives him a playful smack. Gry laughs. Karen steps in front of Quince, and he lets himself speak to her as he sees her, elevated, his knight.

'May I?'

She puts her hands on her hips, closes her eyes.

Quince draws a silvery moustache over her Cupid's bow. She walks down to the lake to consider her reflection in the water, hands in her jacket pockets.

'It suits me!'

'It really does,' Gry says, taking Adam's arm.

'Adam needs some make-up too!'

Adam makes a face. Quince mimics him.

'This really isn't necessary,' Adam says.

'Don't be so boring,' Gry says.

Quince feels his pulse quicken, takes a deep breath. He's standing in front of Adam, and they're almost the same height. Quince traces his fingertips along Adam's high cheekbones, up to his ear, slowly down to his mouth; Adam turns away.

'That's fine.'

Quince looks at Gry, who rolls her eyes. Quince shrugs, takes Charlie's hand, escorts her over to Sylvia. Esben sits on Sylvia's other side (well, that was easy, Quince thinks).

They try to settle among the pillows, the Romanesque landscape. Sylvia leans on an arm, half reclined. Come on, this is her natural habitat. And at the same time, she's on edge. It's too quiet. Should they have music on? Would that be too staged? She looks at the platter of crayfish, red and boiled. How perfect that Karen caught them, so scenic and Swedish and summery, Sylvia thinks, but what exactly are you supposed to do with a crayfish? How do you handle it? The friends are waiting, and in the wait the magic

149

falters. As if the whole scene is precisely that. A scene. Here they are in their nice clothes, their sprinkle of glitter paint. Suddenly it dawns on Sylvia that they are the most pretentious people in the world, and she's the most pretentious of them all. This is just a game, something they're playing at. You want to make the set feel real. But crayfish have shells, what the hell is she supposed to do? She casts a desperate look for help. Charlie catches it, places a calming hand on her leg.

'Karen, can you walk us through these crayfish?' Charlie asks.

'Of course! You just shell them, like a prawn or a lobster,' she starts.

Charlie presses her lips together.

'Could you elaborate?'

'Take one, we'll do it together. No, come on, let's sit up, it's so awkward with these pillows,' Karen says. 'Alright. Hold the body between your thumb and fore-finger, and then twist the head off. Exactly! Then press down so it splits open, like with fresh peas. Right, like that. And then twist off the tail.'

Now they're in the picture. Now they're peeling crayfish. Tearing off hunks of bread to dip in the juice dripping from the crustaceans, running over their fingers, sticky. Gry giggles, holding a crayfish out in front of her, cupping her hand beneath it, trying to protect her dress.

'This is so hard!'

It's even better now, Sylvia thinks, that they are in

the idyll but bad at it; they need to say aloud: This is difficult, but we're doing it anyway. They can admit they're playing, but still they're playing.

'You have to get your hands dirty,' Karen says, but she's an expert, and manages to keep her own hands clean through the whole process. Quince laughs, drenched in crayfish juice.

'Go wash off in the lake, kid.' Karen is so imperious that he's up right away, ignoring the impulse to kneel; he loves her tied-back hair and imperatives. He walks down to the lake, drops to his knees in the water, which reaches up to the frayed edges of his shorts. He feels like he's in a music video, boy-band cute, the sunset in the water, the white vest that turns transparent when wet. He splashes water up his arms, cupping his hands like ladles. The crayfish juice spreads from his hands over the surface of the water like a grease stain.

He hears steps behind him. Please don't let it be Adam. He stiffens. Or let it be Adam, he thinks against his will – let him see me being marvellous in the water, in the light, let him be the one to say something.

Adam stays by the shore, washes his hands in silence.

*

Sylvia sighs into her wine glass. How is it possible to be so tense and so relaxed? She reclines slightly, leans her head on Charlie's arm. If she stretches out her leg, she can reach Esben with her foot, his elbow, he's talking to Gry, absently grabs Sylvia's foot, holds it, a thumb on

151

her instep. Oh God. Just stay in it. She's back in her Kelly Taylor fantasy, she's enraptured. Why does this have to affect anyone? Why shouldn't she be lying here, bound to both? No one will lose anything from it. Everything, everything is possible. But oh, how to say it aloud?

Quince returns from the lake, arms outspread.

'What if we all got married?'

Karen grins.

'That's a good offer. But I think you'd have too hard a time being faithful to us.'

Quince sits down.

'I probably would. Have a hard time with it. But seriously. Open relationships are possible – have you ever considered it?'

Sylvia winces: Quince isn't one for subtlety, but fine, now it's out there.

'I mean, it sounds exciting, and it could be fun to sleep around, but I think there's plenty to take care of with one relationship,' Karen says. She doesn't need more emotional labour, more human chaos; maybe she could be like Don Draper in the 1950s, having an affair with a secretary, but she doesn't want a mess, nothing that means anything.

'I don't know if I'd want to sleep around,' Esben says. He doesn't sound offended, just looks pensive, continues: 'But when people talk about open relationships, I always think about Selma Lagerlöf. Do you remember that lecture about Mårbacka? Her house? Lagerlöf wasn't allowed to inherit it, but then she bought it back with her Nobel Prize money. On the top floor, she had this huge library attached to several bedrooms. One for herself. And one for her partner. And one for her other girlfriend, I think. And guest rooms, of course. Have you ever heard anything more fantastic? What an idyllic, beautiful way to live!'

Sylvia loves him for that, for identifying with lesbian women, the red splotches breaking out on his neck. It *is* the most beautiful way of life, a large, shared house *and* a room of one's own, a gigantic library, a collective of clever, sad arty types, who've read all kinds of books, but would gladly read them again. Aloud to each other. We could help each other to write all our books and pay visits to each other's rooms in long nightgowns or nightshirts with a candle in hand; the image weaves inside her, she already has a long white nightgown; it's perfect.

'When you win a Nobel Prize someday, please let me be the one to invest the money,' Karen says. They all laugh, Esben too. Sylvia wants to scream, flip the platter of crayfish; finally, there was a fantasy on the table with room for all of them.

'Or we could live like Tove Jansson and Tuulikki Pietilä, each in our own apartments with our own studios, connected by corridors – isn't that the dream?' Quince suggests.

'But they probably only lived like that because they couldn't get married,' Charlie interjects. Sylvia doesn't know what she's going to say, something reactionary in her wants to go back to a time when she and Charlie couldn't, weren't allowed to live together, where something in society would be holding her back, instead of her own hesitancy.

Karen clears her throat.

'I mean, I personally have no interest in living in a collective. I realise that everyone has a sex drive, of course you have crushes on other people, but if you have an open relationship, then your partner is also allowed to sleep with other people, and then it stops there.'

'Does it?' Quince asks. 'Isn't that a little immature? That no one can play with my things? If I had a significant other, I would want them to have the whole world. I wouldn't want to deny him or her or them anything. And whenever I'm with someone who has a significant other, I'm not taking anything from them.'

Karen smiles: 'But you don't have a significant other. You never do. And maybe you should stop going around and stealing everyone else's.'

'Hey, I'm not stealing! I'm . . . a supplement!'

They all laugh.

'What if it wasn't just about sex? What if it was about love?' Sylvia asks. 'If it wasn't about fulfilling a physical need, if it was about being able to feel something for multiple people at the same time, wouldn't it be a kind of utopia if . . .'

'That just seems so messy and chaotic,' Karen says. 'And for that matter, love and sex are so valuable, so intimate. It's rare that it just works, and when you find that, you want to protect it, the relationship. You could argue that monogamy is superior, to sanctify one single person to the exclusion of all others. That's what makes it special.'

'Well, yes, but a slutty Marxist would call that artificial scarcity. Maybe it's just false consciousness, that you need to be stingy with sex and love because sex and love are rare, but sex and love are rare because we're so stingy with them,' Quince says.

Adam gets involved.

'All that polyamory business, isn't it just communism for people who are too horny to read political theory? And it's not true that sex isn't scarce. Not only for incels, for all of us. Everything is scarce. It's naïve to believe otherwise. The essence of reality is scarcity, as Sartre writes. There isn't enough love, enough food, enough goodness for everyone to have what they want. There's nowhere near enough time to do everything we want. Everyone wants something, and there isn't enough for everyone. We always have a deficit. The passive version of deficit is yearning. And the active version is conflict.'

Something in Sylvia deflates. Oh no, that's how it is, so she's doomed to her daydreams, to yearning – it will never become a reality.

Quince shrugs.

'Sartre was polyamorous, bro.'

Gry snorts. She places a hand on Quince's shoulder.

'I think it would be exciting. But Adam would never,' she says.

Adam winks, mimics Gry: 'I also think it would be exciting. But Gry would never.'

Gry laughs again. She feels so light and free. The reeds are heaving, the night is long, the sky keeps being bright. Should we take a little MDMA next time? she wonders. Some shroom tea? Gry is surprised to hear her mum-voice suggest it, the voice that anticipates a need in the group, before the others have noticed, the same inner voice that reminds her to put the kettle on. Maybe it could be on the agenda for next time, maybe the kids could stay at home, and she can see it, looking out on the lake: a bowl, between the reeds, in the sunset water, a glittering red punch, promising to raise them up to a heavenly place.

Charlie's voice is loud and clear.

'I would never be able to have an open relationship. No way. I'm way too jealous, and I'm okay with that.'

She's so attractive, Gry thinks to her surprise; it's precisely that faithfulness, the jealousy in Charlie that's so magnetic. And those shoulders, my God.

Gry looks out at the reeds, while the others keep talking; she thinks she senses the lights that supposedly belonged to ghost ships on the lake and lured people astray. It feels like a long time since she's last been among adults, at a party, out without her kids. For once she feels the children tighten around her, even though they've behaved enormously well. She wants to stay up late, she wants to turn off the quiet buzzing in the back of her head, at the periphery of her field of vision, that is always calculating the level of danger. She is tired, she realises; for five years she's been calculating risk: are those rice cakes too salty, is the tree too tall to climb, and if she calls Vera down from a dry, dead beech branch, will she break her adventurous spirit, damage her confidence?

Does she like being a mum, or is she just good at it, and it's nice to do things that you're good at, instead of needing to make an effort all the time?

Her head is buzzing, her legs prickling with heat.

'I'll grab some more wine.'

She needs to see the kids. Be close to them and recalibrate, remember her love, its simplicity. It's cool and dark in the kids' room. She sits on the edge of the bottom bunk. Vera has thrown her leg over the duvet; children's limbs are so free in their sleep. Their freedom, their worriless life is conditioned on her constant attention. The children give her life purpose, yes, but they are also the opposite of freedom. For a moment she wishes that they weren't there.

Gry gets up. Sejr's bunk is empty.

She lifts the duvet bunched at the foot of the bed – is he underneath? Is he breathing? But he's not there. She looks around in the dark, in Vera's bed, in their double bed. Turns on the light, Vera rolls over in her sleep. He's not there.

*

'Sejr is missing.'

Adam's face goes blank; he's up right away. He goes into their room, which Gry has just searched, and she hopes that he'll somehow find Sejr there anyway, that his sense of order will trump the disorder of the world.

Adam returns, pallid, shakes his head. The conversation has stopped.

'I thought you were watching them?' Adam says.

Karen gets up, says sharply: 'What kind of thing is that to say? They're your kids too.'

Karen takes Gry's hand.

'Come on, let's look inside.'

They go back in. Karen notices the back door is ajar.

Oh no, Gry thinks. He must have woken up; he must have crawled out the bed. She pictures his hesitant feet, he wanted to sleep on top, he's only three, wanting to take in the whole world without being able to assess the risk, and I was just sitting there, having a nice time, drinking wine, thinking about a big red punchbowl in the reeds. Maybe he woke up and got scared, maybe he was calling me, but I couldn't hear him. I said we were outside, now he's wandered into the woods alone.

Karen gets a torch from the shed. They agree to split up and meet back at the house in fifteen minutes. It's dark. They're immediately sober. Serious faces with traces of face paint. Gry looks between the roots, looks out on the glassy water. What if he fell into the lake? Here, in the midnight woods, she feels in her body what the creatures from her research have come from.

A need for monsters in the darkness, that they had to invent creatures to explain the terror that seizes you at night, to explain where disappeared children go, that they are lured away by elves, tricked. What if he waded into the water, sleepy and afraid? She can see it: the lifeless body drifting in the dark water. Limp, heavy, like Vera's sleepy surrender in her bunk.

She doesn't want to, but she thinks: He's dead. He's already dead. What if she has to spend the rest of her life as a mother who has lost her child? She tries to keep her senses open, scouting between the trunks; was that a sound in the woods, is he out there somewhere, is he calling her?

'Sejr!' she calls, terrified by how thin her voice sounds.

The thoughts are familiar: having children means imagining losing them over and over again. Falling and hurting themselves, knocking out teeth, falling and puncturing a lung on a vertical branch in the woods, getting kidnapped, someone abusing them, before killing them. Better the woods, in that case, she thinks to herself.

She chews her cheek, feeling the calm pressure of her molars against her skin, it's difficult to focus.

But it's true, her racing mind insists, having children means imagining, repeatedly, how they will be torn from you, until it seems incomprehensible that they could ever die. Aren't they in mortal danger every day? Isn't it statistically improbable that we can protect them? They demand such constant attention, such faithful protection. Sometimes she sees Sejr and Vera's entire childhoods before her, as if they were walking ahead of her, through tall grass, their large heads swaying on their thin necks, fragile as poppies, and you have the impulse to reach out, to put a protective hand on the backs of their heads. There is something almost provocative about their defencelessness, because it makes one imagine the attack.

She shakes her head, sniffs. Illuminates the space between the beech roots, the moss shining all too greenly back at her; outside the perimeter of light the forest is dark and buzzing. She doesn't want to be without her children, she just wants to find Sejr. She promises a God she doesn't believe in that if Sejr comes back to her, she'll always look after him.

There's something inside you – her thoughts continue about her poppy-like children – that wants to be crushed, yes, that wants to be changed forever; you want to be tragic, you want to stop speaking, you want to be bereaved, and wouldn't a small part of you also be relieved? So, then you could finally let go, stop fearing the threat, because it would once and for all have become a reality.

But I have two children, she drily reminds her brain. I would have to keep going, suffer on, while fearing even more for my living child.

But, her thoughts whisper, isn't there a small part of you that, secretly, would accept that tinge of trauma, of loss, which would settle over you, which would be grateful for finally seeming interesting, unambiguously, undeniably interesting? No one could call you average.

'Sejr!'

The forest doesn't answer.

She looks at her watch; it's time to go back to the others. They turn back one by one, each of them empty-handed.

'It's not so cold that it's dangerous to be in the woods at night. But maybe we should call the rangers? Because of the lake,' Karen says.

Sylvia notices that Esben has fallen back. He's pale. A nervous hand at his temple, like a broken salute, as if he is swatting something away. He goes into the house, she follows him. The others can make the call. Esben leans against the doorway to the living room, his eyes are closed, his hands over his face, he's taking deep breaths through his nose, sniffs. His hands waver as if there were threads in them.

She takes a step towards him.

'Hey. Everything will be okay. We'll find him.'

Esben looks at her, but as if he doesn't see her. She takes one of his wavering hands: 'Come here. Let's sit.'

He shakes his head. Shuts his eyes again. His hands tremble in hers.

'Yes, come here. It's okay.'

Sylvia is assertive, to her own surprise.

'Now, let's relax.'

She holds his hand, puts her other hand at his side,

as if they were dancing, as if he's an older man she has to support, she can feel a proud, upright feeling inside her, she likes feeling strong; with him, she can be the one to lead.

'Let's just sit down for a second.'

He nods. She leads him to the green sofa in the corner. She squeezes his hand. He squeezes back. His breathing deepens, calms. He leans his head against hers. They could stay like this forever. His breath is warm on her neck. Then they look down. There, on the sofa, Sejr is sound asleep.

Day 6

Today, they're getting ready. They are still rattled, still relieved that no tragedy happened the night before. They're taking care of the last few things, trying to shake off Sejr's disappearance.

They'll go to bed early tonight, sober, to be rested for the morning. Karen delegates tasks at breakfast. But nearly everything has been taken care of, her parents are bringing a wedding arch for the ceremony, food, her dad's gigantic paella pan; it'll be a crayfish massacre. Quince heard someone fucking last night, has no idea who. Gry is floating around, she kisses Adam's head as he puts on his sunglasses.

Quince reclines in his chair, contemplates a peach. It is wet and juicy. He loves stone fruits, but the juice is a recurring issue, they're so hard to eat neatly. He eats slowly, a drop of juice escapes, runs down over his chin. He ignores the impulse to wipe off the juice, let him be garish; takes another bite and feels the stream grow, over his chest, belly skin; he leans back, shuts his eyes and feels the trail of juice like a chill on his skin, the sun warming the stickiness, but it can't dry it up; the drop reaches the reddish hair beneath his navel, which is downy, but from the perspective of the drop it's a crevice and the drop is insistent, doesn't stick but sidles from one hair to the next, until it finds the sky-blue seam of his denim shorts, sinks in, blossoms into a dark little stain.

Adam gets up, gathers his things, gives Gry a quick kiss. Is he about to work, answer emails? He pauses by Quince's lounge chair.

'Does everything have to be a show with you?' he asks, before going inside.

Quince doesn't know if it was a joke, how to respond. He blinks, nauseated, the fruit suddenly wrong in his stomach.

It's too much. Quince is baking in the sun and from the inside. Adam is so straight, so foreign, he doesn't have the energy to compete, to try to be seen, Quince doesn't know what to do with himself, he wants to escape and scream into a pillow for a hundred years.

He ends up screaming into a pillow. But first. He's back in his room, lying on his bed, partially undressed (something inside him loves the scene, seeing himself from the outside, with his clothes a mess, unbuttoned jeans, open shirt, as if someone was hurrying to get to his body). He wants to turn the ache into pure horniness, something that can be released.

He gives himself permission, imagines Adam, tries to conjure up something rough, he usually likes that. But instead, he imagines a bright landscape of sheets, late morning sun, cooler, fresher than the heat here, an open window, a Sunday, a glass of orange juice on a sunny table. And Adam. What does that mean? Maybe he's not really in the mood after all.

But then: he feels the nerve endings in his body like small dogs smelling blood.

Okay, Quince tries distrustfully, hesitantly, spits into his hand, dips his fingers into the spit, before touching himself: a weekend morning, Adam, his sleepy face, a warmth to his smile, his upper body, but especially his face, the sun in his stubble when he smiles.

Excuse me?

Quince argues with his body, his brain, his impulses, tells them that they're off-base, domesticating Adam, there's no reason to do that, he assures himself, don't I like him because he's a beast? But no, his body responds, and the sunshine ripples through him, lifts him up, seizes his spine; you want him to know you, you want to know each other, to be part of his everyday, and he thinks you're clever, he thinks you're dumb because he knows you, and you sleep in together, and you wake up together, and you drink orange juice on a Sunday morning. Quince feels the waves in his body, contracting in him; the images fade into one another, Adam, leaning in over him, holding him, the glass of orange juice, cool and bright in the sun. The orgasm comes over him before he realises what's happened; he turns over, an almost scared scream into the pillow.

It's worse than he thought.

Sylvia is going to kill him.

*

Karen scrutinises the scarlet wedding cake. Dark berry mousse, a towering arrangement. She looks up, notices Sylvia standing in the doorway.

'It's not exactly my forte. Gry would have made something better,' Karen says.

She hesitantly takes a box of macarons in a matching dark purple, and she positions them around the side of the cake, smushing them into the soft mousse. It feels gelatinous, it feels like a waste of her time. She wants to give up, turns to Sylvia, throwing up her hands.

'It's supposed to look like the cake we used to get at La Glace, but it looks like I've decorated it with butt plugs.'

Sylvia giggles.

'Wow, I didn't think you had it in you!'

'As one says,' Karen winks drily.

Sylvia laughs, but then she looks down at the floor, shuffles out of the room.

Karen watches her go, washes her hands. She thinks about the old days. About how close she and Sylvia used to be. They saw something in one another, a natural egoism, a main character syndrome; it was liberating how they didn't need to worry about being nice, they only cared about being intelligent, debating, excelling.

They were ambitious, vain, let each other be it. She's always telling herself that she needs alone time, but she knows she misses Sylvia.

They used to tease Esben, talked about his seriousness, his thoughtful pauses, his ethics, how he never said anything wrong, never said anything banal, that it was insufferable; they conspired in the student bar; what if we pretend to have understood a poem, a film, an ethical dilemma exactly opposed to him, would that ruffle him? They never managed to.

The three of them had had an intuitive interest in one another. In the beginning they tried to impress, to perform for each other, they showed each other their favourite films; she had shown them *Reprise*, a mirror, a group of young friends dreaming about writing, competing, playing smart, falling in love; Esben had covered his eyes when Philip, who becomes a successful writer, had a psychotic episode, lost his grasp on reality. Karen had thought that he was delicate; it awoke something in her, a protective instinct.

Esben had fallen asleep after putting on his favourite film. Karen and Sylvia had struggled to hold back their laughter. When the film was over, the DVD started up once more; Karen and Sylvia looked at each other: 'Should we watch it again?' Sylvia asked; neither of them had understood it, but if they watched it again, maybe they had a chance? Sylvia was so obsessed with understanding things correctly; would she really watch a film twice to not feel stupid? It had always been easier for Karen to reject things she didn't have a taste for, an instinctive sense of what she liked. But they let the film continue, they ended up in a fit of laughter, the long Swedish silences, as soon as someone giggles, the game is over, when the women's grave faces melted together in the summerhouse mirror: they couldn't restrain themselves anymore, they woke Esben with their laughter. He looked confused, from them to the women onscreen to the clock on the wall. Got up to write something down, smiled. They hadn't understood the film the second time they saw it either, but they knew that they cared about Esben and his seriousness and boringness. And that they cared for each other.

Slowly, they started to relax. They shared the sofa, all three of them, watched American television series; Sylvia and Karen would fire off sloppy analyses, Esben would try to say something comprehensive, clear, they would boo him; he gave up, mild as always, refilling their drinks.

She and Sylvia were on the same wavelength, but they weren't the same. Sylvia was and is full of life, with her almost Pixar-animated face, always smiling and laughing, which makes it seem like she's always happy – and yet, Karen thinks, you can feel that she isn't. We think that people who are sweet and funny are happy because they smile a lot, she thinks to herself. But there's a melancholy to Sylvia, a sadness that she ought to take seriously. It's a gendered problem. Gry is the same way. She looks down at her belly, the fabric is covered in dark-purple stains, and she promises herself that if she is pregnant, if she has a daughter, she'll teach her not to cultivate sweetness like a cardinal virtue, not to smile unless she's actually happy.

But she and Sylvia had something special. What happened to their friendship? Karen is closer to Gry now, because she's always there, always replies to her messages.

Now she's missing Sylvia's impulses to say something toxic, funny, instead of constantly affirming the idyll. Karen senses that Sylvia still has it buried in her, her own view on things. She would like to talk to her about whether it makes sense to have kids; she already knows that Gry would propagandise them.

She misses her friend. She knows that she can be distant too, secluded, but she wishes that someone would come to find her.

When did their friendship become so polite, so perfunctory? Why did she just leave?

*

Esben and Gry are making dinner. He inhales through his nose, puts an arm around her.

'Don't worry, I'm okay,' Gry says. 'Just think that you found him, that he wasn't even gone. But . . .' She shakes her head; she can't find the words. Esben seems to understand. She takes a deep breath.

'I felt so bad because we were just having a nice time. I hadn't even noticed him get up. It's like, even if you let go for just a moment, something terrible can happen.'

He squeezes her shoulders.

'Don't blame yourself. You're the best mum in the world.'

Gry wriggles her way out, she goes to wipe the table. Esben shifts on his feet. Gry can immediately tell when someone wants to say something.

'Is something wrong?' she asks.

Esben hesitates, puts a hand to his mouth, looks up. Gry gives him time, she keeps her eyes on the cloth, moves a glass. Esben is so sublime and mystical, and he's also just a little boy, she thinks, who's never learned to confide in someone.

'Yes, well. Sorry for talking about myself now, that's not what this is about. It's just . . . I see how good you are at being a parent. You're phenomenal. And I just don't know whether I can have a kid . . . if I could handle it, I mean.'

'Darling, you'd be such a good father.'

He looks at her, mild, telling. Then she understands. She read his book, about his mother, his childhood; it's genetic, he must be afraid of passing it on.

'Oh, Esben.'

He picks at his cuticles.

'Are you thinking about having kids?' Gry asks.

He shifts around on his sandals, embarrassed to be talking about himself.

'I thought a lot about it while I was writing. I feel like I've been holding my breath for months. I really want to. But my gene pool isn't exactly ideal.'

Gry is overwhelmed by an urge to embrace him. Wave it away, assure him that he has nothing to be afraid of, smooth things out. But his serious eyes. She can feel how real it is for him. She takes his hand.

'It's good of you to think so much about it, very noble . . .'

Esben clicks his tongue, a tsk, his voice is sharper than usual.

'No, it's not. It's not some kind of cross I'm bearing. It's a grief, but it's like it is a form of grief that has always been there, woven inside me, I've always thought that I wouldn't have children.'

Gry holds his hand. She's not afraid of his mood, she just listens.

'But now I think for the first time that maybe I do . . . want to. I want to, so much, it's almost nauseating. But can I? Is it just some form of narcissism? You only have kids for yourself.'

Gry clears her throat.

'Sorry!'

'No, it's true.'

She squeezes his hand.

'Have you talked to Karen about how you feel?' Gry asks.

'Of course, thank goodness for Karen. It's easier to trust her perception of the world than my own. She's so solid. She would be fine, no doubt, but I don't know if she wants kids as much as I do.'

'Maybe she doesn't need to?'

Gry steadies herself, it feels invasive to wade into his head like this.

'If you let yourself be a little selfish . . . because you know, everyone is allowed to be selfish sometimes . . . having kids can also be healing. Doing things totally differently to how your parents did, taking responsibility, breaking patterns. You can do it. You're not a child, you're an adult. When I see you now, you're clearly in a much better place than when we were at university. You take care of yourself. You're more relaxed, at ease with who you are. You don't have all those little tics anymore.'

Esben smiles down at his sandals.

'Writing has helped a lot. And talking to someone . . . Things are also better with my mum,' he says quietly. 'I'm better. That's part of what fucks me up. I'm better, but at the same time I'm always going to feel bad. What if I have a kid who feels the same way? It was so scary when I was younger.'

He's looking straight at her now.

'I know, it's difficult,' Gry responds. 'And there will be things that will be more challenging for you. And you'll have to make sure you get enough sleep,' she emphasises. 'But that doesn't mean that you can't be a wonderful parent. Your genes, and your brain chemistry, are incredible too, you know. And you have us. We'll all be there for you. You can be totally out of it *and* be there for your kids *and* be okay. You would take such good care of a child . . . and you would be so tuned into how they were doing, if they were having a hard time. And who knows, maybe you'll have a boring, *basic*, neurotypical kid.'

He swings her hand in his.

'You're such a forcefield,' he says. 'Sorry for being such a weeping willow.'

She doesn't know how to respond. She smiles. She can't help herself; she makes a joke, trying to lift them out of this heaviness; in an exaggeratedly stern tone, hands on her hips, she reprimands him: 'Now, let's not be those millennials who think everything is danger-ous for kids. Our parents were ice cold, they never used seatbelts or went to therapy. And you know, we turned out fine, right?'

Esben snorts, wiggling his hand in the air to say so-so.

*

Sylvia is restless, she doesn't know what to do. She notices a fig tree in the distance, silver bark and even branches. A climbing tree. It's easy to climb, even in a long dress. She sits in a nook, where the trunk spreads into branches, into a crown, into a heavenly swirl of figs. This is just like *The Bell Jar*, Sylvia thinks, when the main character is sitting in a fig tree, and every fruit represents a possible future, infinite dreams. But the figs here are light green and unripe.

One fig is a little family, dressing infants in precious

wool, breastfeeding them, falling asleep knowing that you'll have enough comfort and worry for a lifetime, that you've settled.

Another fig is a noble loneliness, living the consequences of always being prickly about everything and everyone, wanting to have it all, saying no, retreating, sitting at a desk in a ray of sunshine, working seriously, ascetic, devoting oneself to something other than yearning.

A third fig is the dream of a community, travelling, but where? To Berlin, New York? Not looking back, keeping the company of trans dream princes and bisexual drama queens, a life of kink bars and poetry readings, where you greet each other with a kiss on the mouth, knowing the people on your street. Let escapism become the everyday, a neighbourhood. She looks longingly at that fig. Couldn't she and Quince do it: make their own home somewhere instead of living in this straight world?

One fig is running away, one fig is Charlie, one fig is Esben . . .

Sylvia looks up, out over the lake. Adam is swimming laps. She rests her head on the tree trunk and watches him. Long strokes, almost professional.

Why not – another fig could be Adam; how would she grow with someone like him? Would she be more secure, more at ease with normality, would she start keeping up with the news, start feeling healthy, solid, vigorous, like a real world-historical subject?

But in *The Bell Jar*, it dawns on Sylvia with a sinking feeling, the girl in the tree is doomed to die of hunger, enamoured and confused by all the figs, but unable to choose one of them because it would exclude the others; instead, she sits there, paralysed, watches each fig rot, wither and fall as she herself disappears. Adam, the Bogart philosopher, would say that you need to do something, choose one or the other, figure it out, act, instead of sitting there rotting.

Sylvia is comfortable up in the tree, secure; she closes her eyes.

But why is it so easy for everyone to be satisfied with their own figs?

She lets the images fade into each other as the light flickers through the leaves, she can see it through her eyelids.

She starts when she feels a cold hand around her foot.

Adam is standing under the tree, dripping wet.

'What are you doing? Are you taking a nap?'

'I'm Sylvia Plath.'

'C'mon. Get down.'

She dramatically slides down the trunk; he catches her, puts her down on the ground, keeps his hands on her shoulders. He's so tall, she thinks in a daze. He is wearing swim trunks and lake water. Some glitter from the previous night flashes on his cheek. She doesn't know what to say. Decides to be quiet, to wait and see what he does. She wakes up when he lets a finger rest against her breastbone: 'You've got to stop this depressive shit. Try reading something that wasn't written by women writers who killed themselves.'

She shivers. She loves being told what to do. Though it won't help her figure out what to do.

He looks down at her.

'Think like a normal person,' he says, slowly and clearly.

He starts to walk back up to the house.

'Adam.'

He stops, turns back to her.

'Honestly. You seem so solid all the time. How do you do it? Do you ever feel fucked up or confused or sad?'

'Nope. It's pure stasis in here.'

She considers that. 'You know, the word "stasis" means civil war.'

*

'It's been such a wonderful week,' Gry says. 'You couldn't have planned it better; it's been so nice getting to just be together, and the weather has been perfect. And nothing went wrong,' she says, looking at Esben.

Something in Sylvia slips. She speaks louder than she means to: 'Actually, I agree with Quince. I think we should all marry each other. What if we just stayed here, and things could always be like this? We could be more intimate.'

Gry laughs.

'Yeah, totally.'

'Seriously, I mean it. I want you all back. I miss us. I don't want to go back to real life. I don't just want a little life and an apartment and coupledom and kids and the everyday stress. Do you?'

The table is quiet.

'Is that really what all of you want?'

'Chill,' Adam says.

Sylvia wants to scream. They're all too relaxed. She runs her fingers through her hair, closes her eyes. She can't take it anymore.

'What are we so afraid of? Why have these boundaries, why insist on the difference between sex and love, friends and lovers, friendship and desire? As if.'

Gry surveys the group.

'I think we're all a little worn out. We've been in such close proximity to each other the past few days. Maybe we need a little space,' she starts.

Charlie is staring at Sylvia, brows furrowed.

'Is this really how you feel?' she asks in a quiet voice.

Sylvia reaches for her hand, but Charlie crosses her arms, stares down at her plate.

'I think that we all feel that way, even though we don't admit it. If we let ourselves, we could experience all kinds of love. It's so greedy . . . no, dumber than greed: it's a waste of resources. We could be living this utopian life together, but instead . . . you have to choose between loneliness or a twosome, which is the same as loneliness. Besides, everyone cheats, everyone breaks the rules. Monogamy is a religion that no one can live up to, but no one dares to leave behind.'

The table is quiet. Karen speaks, her voice calm and clear.

'If it worked in practice, don't you think more people would be living that way? The majority of people couple off and have nuclear families for a reason . . .'

'It's only because we're all following each other, the same homogenous norms,' Sylvia responds.

'That's not true,' Adam says. 'Everything is so free now. You can be as queer and polyamorous as you please. It isn't society's fault that everyone doesn't want to fuck you.'

'Well, that's just hopelessly heteronormative of you,' Quince says.

Sylvia catches his eye; thank God, at least he gets it. Esben looks like he's trying to grasp what is happening. He is quiet, but Sylvia can see a vein flickering in his neck. She softens her tone: 'Don't you ever have feelings for your friends that you don't know what to do with?' she asks, looking at Esben.

'I mean, it's a nice thought,' Esben starts.

'No, it isn't,' Karen says, resting her hand on his. 'I don't need any more love, any more intimacy. I don't need any more feelings in my life. Honestly, there are other things I'd rather spend my time and energy on. Why does everything have to be so alternative and complicated? Have you considered the consequences, if we all slept with everyone? Why do we have to be so obsessed with love, when we could be focusing on what we're doing with our lives, with the state of the world? Why not spend our energy on something *useful*?'

Sylvia wants to whisper that she isn't talking to Karen.

'I can't believe you're bringing this up right now,' Charlie says, her gaze fixed on the table, avoiding Sylvia's eyes. Gry reaches over, puts a hand on her shoulder.

'I don't think so,' Adam says flatly. 'I think it's intriguing. Completely unrealistic and immature but intriguing. I think I would be fine with Gry sleeping with another woman, but . . .'

'Thanks for that, Adam,' Karen snaps. 'And by the way, that's sexist. It's like saying that women don't count. Would you only sleep with men, then?'

Adam shrugs.

Charlie stands up, faces Sylvia.

'Normal people get jealous when their girlfriends sleep with other people. Wouldn't you be upset if I slept with someone else?'

Sylvia looks up at the sky.

'No, I'd think it was fantastic that there was more love in the world. I think it's stingy to deprive someone else of something wonderful just because of your own feelings.'

Sylvia is getting carried away, feeling self-righteous, telling them off. She doesn't register Quince trying to catch her eye, making a gesture with his hand over his throat, *cut*, doesn't register Charlie turning to leave. Karen smiles, close-lipped, at her plate, pale with anger.

'Sylvia, *you* are the most self-centred person here. We're here because Esben and I are getting married tomorrow, or have you forgotten that?'

'Well, you didn't tell us this was going to be a wedding. Honestly, I'm disappointed. It's so predictable.'

She wrings her hands.

'Is this really what you want? Don't you want more from life?'

'That's not any of your business,' Karen says. 'You can do whatever you want. No one's stopping you, but all you do is talk shit about how everyone else is living their lives.'

You are stopping me, Sylvia thinks, but it's bigger than that.

'The whole world is stopping me, and you know that. Of course, you can go out and meet new people and hook up with them but I don't care about random people. I care about you all, my friends; you're the ones that I love, that I miss. I have fifteen years of feelings saved up for you all. I thought we'd be building our lives together. I'm just fed up with the total lack of fantasy. In theory, we can do everything, but in practice everyone just does the same thing. Gets married, has kids, a mortgage. Next thing, you'll be pregnant too.'

Karen's face falls; she looks hurt for real. *Is* she pregnant? Sylvia is shocked but not surprised: it's easy to play the prophet when everyone is so predictable.

The air is thick, still.

'So, which of us do you want to sleep with then?' Adam asks with a grin.

'Shut up,' Sylvia says, covering her face, her burning cheeks.

Suddenly, she's exhausted, by her stubbornness, her immaturity, by how she's pushing them away, but especially by the fact that she just can't articulate herself well enough to make them understand. That she loves them, that she needs them. She wishes she were more eloquent, so that she could dazzle them all, convince them, but concepts, theories of love are impossible. Everything you can say out loud sounds so dumb. In her mind, it's crystal clear: sitting on a veranda with Charlie, in their old age, knitting, steady hands; they'd have children, so many children, already grown, starting their own lives. They would have wild, wanton sex, even though they were old, matronly, a well-kept secret in the mild, lesbian idyll; a charming antique dresser full of leather, chains, sky-blue strap-ons; they'd fuck each other sore and happy, and then go outside to watch the sunset in the trees. But first: a sprawling, open youth. Maybe she would wake up in another bed, with Esben and Karen, be part of what they have? She would wake up while they slept, watch the sunrise through a window other than her own. Maybe she and Karen would rediscover the special bond they used to have?

'You know, Sylvia, not everyone is going around

with complexes, suffering from false consciousness, and it's pretty arrogant to assume they are,' Karen says.

'That's even worse, you've chosen to be mediocre of your own free will. I'm so fucking done with your organic vanilla hetero-banality,' Sylvia scoffs.

She pushes back her chair. She has to find Charlie. Charlie is standing by the lake. Smoking. She pouts like a child when she's angry, when she's upset; there's something defiant about her mouth. She has never been more beautiful, enraged in the evening light, in the breeze. I take her for granted, and I will again, Sylvia thinks.

Charlie, who pretends to have a short fuse, a fiery temper, out of love, when they're fooling around, but now, for once, she's furious. She's had enough.

Something in Sylvia thinks: Just murder me with your rage, won't you. Go Othello on me. This would be a fine place to end.

But it's worse than that. They have to talk.

Sylvia is afraid of Charlie's real feelings: how pure and clear they are. Charlie's plot is simple, sure, Steven Spielberg, while she is a cerebral clutter of repressed daydreams, abstraction to the third degree, a series of hypotheticals.

They've been so afraid to talk about the future. To say it aloud: Sylvia can't see herself in the life that Charlie wants. Chaos and order. Instead, they've been distracting each other with the most mind-blowing sex of their lives.

Charlie knows what she wants, and it's terrifying. Sylvia has prevaricated, formulating the problem internally, reformulating it, and now they're here, standing by the lake.

'Charlie.'

Sylvia makes an effort to speak truthfully.

'I love you.'

Charlie's face contorts in anger, like skin contracting in cold water.

'But you would rather live a life where you date and fuck and fall in love with whoever.'

A pause.

'Well, yes. I think that would be ideal. But I also want you. I love you.'

'You said that. But I can't do this. You know how I am.'

'I know, but I would always come home to you. I want to make a home with you, and we could have kids, and I would be so sweet and calm, if I could just . . .'

'Who exactly do you want to sleep with? Is it Esben?'

A crimson wave crashes over Sylvia's cheeks. How does she know? Does everyone know? She forces herself not to dwell on the shame, the embarrassment, not to ask if it's that obvious. She has some tact.

'Well, yeah . . . but it could be anyone,' she assures Charlie, without knowing whether it's true or strategically smart to say. It seems like the wrong time to name names.

Charlie is incredulous.

'Do you realise how crazy this is? You're acting as if it's totally normal to say: Hey, by the way, I want to have sex with other people. It's so selfish. You are so, insanely, selfish. It's the same when we have sex. I have never met a bigger pillow princess in my life. You don't do anything. You are the greediest person I know.'

Sylvia feels the humiliation welling up. She thought that Charlie loved how acquiescent she was; it wasn't because she was lazy. Sylvia sniffs, she can't hold it back.

'I don't know what I'd do without you,' she says.

'Okay, but then you need to get your shit together. What exactly do you want?'

'. . .'

'And not making a decision is a choice too.'

'People say that, but it's not true. A choice is a choice. Ambivalence is ambivalence. All I have is doubt. It's the only feeling I trust. I can't choose one thing and really mean it. I know I'm the worst, I know my love is useless. I . . .'

'Stop. Just stop talking. I'll choose for you. Seriously, you're the biggest liar in the world. Suddenly you come up with this whole polyamorous worldview, just because you have a crush on your friend, or you realise that you're in love with your friend because you don't believe in monogamy. And you don't even know which is the real reason and which is the excuse. And now you're just standing here, saying this all as if it weren't totally insane to ask me whether you can sleep with other people.'

Charlie is cold, but then she softens.

'Listen: I love you too. I love you so much. All I want is to be with you for the rest of my life. But then I see other people, like Esben and Karen, getting married, choosing each other, and I know deep down that you're never going to love me that way. I can't keep wasting my life. I want a family, I want someone who *wants* to build a home, a life, together with me. You're never going to choose me and be okay with it. Commit. Even if you had your affairs on the side, I still don't think it would be enough. And regardless, I need to be with someone who chooses me over their stupid crushes and fantasies; someone who respects me.'

That Night

Gry strokes Charlie's hair. She's been crying, she's almost asleep, spent from the emotion. Charlie is warm, her ears bright red and wet, boiling like a child. Gry pats her hair, maternally. Again, and again.

Charlie was ready to drive off into the night. Gry stopped her, stony: 'Give me your keys. I know, but you're not driving anywhere. You've been drinking.'

Now they're lying in Gry and Adam's bed. Earlier, Gry was holding Sylvia's shoulders, telling her that everything would be okay. Sylvia was upset, needed to be comforted. Gry and Quince reassured her that it wasn't so bad. Just wait until the morning. Charlie could sleep in Gry and Adam's room tonight. Right? Gry asked Adam with serious eyes.

'Sure. I'll just sleep with Sylvia then.' And she smacked him playfully in the back of the head, covering her mouth with her other hand, unable to suppress a smile. Adam took Gry's hand. Of course, he would sleep on the sofa; he'd do the dishes too. Karen and Esben had already gone to bed.

Gry is proud of herself, of Adam, how they take care

of things, even when a bomb goes off. But what bad timing, seriously . . . the night before the wedding.

Charlie said so too, repeatedly, as she cried to Gry.

'How could she say that? How could she do this . . . in front of everyone . . . tonight of all nights?'

What does Gry think? Sylvia is awkward, inconsiderate, but Gry isn't upset. Not for real. If she's being honest, she would like to be a little freer. Does she get jealous? Not really. She wouldn't mind that much if Adam slept with other people. She could also imagine sleeping with someone else. As long as they knew that they were a family, agreeing they weren't going anywhere. What would be the harm? The thought excites her. She imagines taking the car and driving off with Charlie. Returning once the rest of them were done making a scene. She feels the weight, the heat, from Charlie, lets it run over her. Though maybe not right now, with her broken heart.

What about Adam? What would he do with his freedom? Would he go after Karen? That would sting; would hurt, would make her feel inferior. Not because they had sex, but because she'll never be Karen.

She notices that Charlie has fallen asleep, the grace of how her body relaxes, softens. It's wonderful to be this close. Charlie is so strong and so vulnerable. Gry shuts her eyes. She's tired too; the pair of them are always taking care of the others; now they can rest, enjoy a little peace.

*

Adam washes the dishes as the rest of the house falls asleep. Quince joins him, helps with the drying, both of them quiet as the pile dwindles.

Maybe if they got to know each other, it would pass, turn out to be an illusion. He would realise Adam is dry, aloof, that he is just fine but not everything Quince has built him up to be. Quince hesitates, absently runs a cloth over a plate.

'Well, that's Sylvia for you,' Quince says.

'Yep.'

'She can be a little dramatic.'

Adam adds a dripping plate to the rack with a smirk.

'Actually, I think she's great.'

Quince looks up.

'Really. Yes! But. What? Do you really think so?'

'I appreciate that she owns up to being exhausted and absurd and wanting it all instead of pretending to be strong and in control. No one else has the nerve to do that.'

Quince is taken aback. Interesting. Well, he has plenty of hysteria to offer. But now he can't find his way out of their understated dynamic. He dries another glass; they're running out of dishes.

'One cigarette wouldn't hurt, right?' Quince tries to sound natural. 'Just to reset.'

'Sure.'

Adam is curt, barely affirmative. He wipes his hands on a tea towel, goes out to the terrace but doesn't stop, keeps walking into the forest, the forest altar. Quince follows.

In the leafy nave, Adam sits on the first bench. Lights two cigarettes, passes one to Quince, who turns the other way. How does Adam manage to make all the clichés work? His expectant eyes, resting on Quince, make him feel like he's onstage. The oak tree is right behind him. Let it be his backbone, he thinks. The dark is denser here, where they are hidden by elder trees, under the moonlight and the last rays from the sun that has now fallen beneath the horizon – what's it called, civil twilight?

'What's up? Did you want to talk about something?'

Adam waits, doesn't elaborate.

Quince shivers. How should he respond? What should he do? What does he want?

'What do you mean?'

'You're just acting like there's something going on.'

Oh, fuck. Does Adam know? Did he notice Quince checking him out, lingering? He feels scarlet spreading across his face, he looks down at himself, the transparent shirt; is his whole body blood-red?

Adam stands up. Is he leaving? Quince is relieved. And yet, something inside him doesn't want him to go.

But Adam doesn't leave. He just stands there, quiet and brutal and bright.

Quince focuses on his breathing. The grass beneath him. The breeze from the lake is cool, his cheeks are tingling red. Maybe it's better this way, Adam noticing, Adam knowing, he has to know. Quince doesn't know how to put it, he feels warm, syrupy. Why is Adam just standing there? Why isn't Quince going back to the house? He stays, feeling like an idiot.

Please, a voice inside him whispers.

And then a breeze rustles through the woods, whooshes through him, his frayed nerves, his self-pity; saying: Come on, if you're not a midsummer night's dream, who is?

As if he ever assesses risk.

Just do it. Be Bogart, be Puck. Same difference.

Just do something.

Quince puts out his hand, palm up.

As if to say: This is an offer.

And over the clearing, the darkness blooms; the summer night is everywhere, surrounded by the wild honeysuckles in their sunset shades, their fragrant smell in the dusk seeming to say: This is an offer, one time only.

Adam takes his hand.

Quince rests his thumb on the back of Adam's hand, light pressure, the accumulated anxiety in the soft part between the thumb and forefinger; no longer a hand-shake but a caress. He takes a step closer.

Where does the courage come from?

He draws the forest in with a breath, elder in his lungs.

Lays a hand on Adam's chest, where his shirt parts.

The heel of his hand on cotton, warm fingertips on skin that is cool in the evening air.

Adam seems as aloof as usual. But his face is open. Quince thinks it's asking: What do you want? Do you want to kiss me?

Quince tries to make his own expression say: I want to be *kissed* (you idiot).

But it won't work. It has to be him.

I can do this.

What's the worst that can happen?

Eternal humiliation.

I can do this.

He leans in; the evening air between them disappears in a kiss.

*

Quince's lips are soft, there's something quivering about him. He smells spiced. This feels insane. Adam is holding his face, feeling his cheekbones and curls in the palms of his hand. His boyishness, soft and jagged, even better than he imagined.

This is new.

There is also something new in him.

He doesn't have a problem with homosexuality, but he has never doubted that he liked women.

But this is an exception; everything about Quince is an exception.

Like a light: first a vague flickering, but then it grew stronger and stronger.

He was caught off guard that morning by Quince sitting in the lake, in the early light, like a creature in one of the Danish Golden Age paintings from Gry's research. An image you want to ruin. And who says *brisk*? Adam jumped in, and as he was on the way out, he noticed Quince in the shallow water with his cranky face, as if he owned the place. And it was hard not to notice him, his chest in the water, wet hair. His mouth, his pout.

Adam couldn't ignore it. He couldn't stand up from the water. It's a simple sense of direction, a very simple compass. You can't argue with an erection, it always knows.

He tried to fix it; he had read somewhere that erections go away if you hold your breath for more than thirty seconds. Resolutely he dived underwater; I'll come up for air when I'm straight again.

It didn't work.

He waited, under the water. Tried to understand. But what is there to understand? Adam doesn't waste time on self-deception. It is how it is. Apparently.

Now his hands are tangled in this beautiful boy's hair. His skin is warm, as if he's blushing with his whole body. Adam breathes him in. His heavy, golden eyelids. He is completely intoxicating.

Technically, this is cheating.

But . . . he wouldn't have gone out here with just anyone. He would never have gone out here. But one step followed the other. He would never have followed

Karen out, Sylvia. That would have felt criminal. It also wouldn't have been worth it. Gry's girlfriends are just like her. And she's the most beautiful, the best of them all.

He doesn't doubt that he loves her.

He shakes her out of his head.

Quince is a different story. He just is.

The others would probably say that he's letting himself do this because Quince is a man, because Quince is trans, that it's some kind of fetish.

But it isn't.

It's because of Quince.

Adam wants to grab him, hard. It isn't theoretical, it has nothing to do with his 'gender identity'. This is physical, and therefore true.

Adam puts a thumb to Quince's chin, opens his mouth slightly, enough to deepen the kiss; a soft noise escapes; it means yes.

It's good to do something, to feel something so real. Adam has been living in this lazy, endless dinner party for days, all the conversations about love and relationships, and what is possible and impossible, pure abstraction, wading through mires of doubt and revolutionary chitchat. So much salon talk, oh, can we be more radical? But none of them would ever consider doing anything in earnest. He agrees with Sylvia, in fact, the idea is interesting, but there's no reason to spiral into an identity crisis. No reason to get so obsessed. And not here, in a summerhouse, in front of your girlfriend. There's no reason to make a scene.

But then, there was Quince (Adam gathers a handful of hair, tugs it lightly). He looks like another life.

A few days ago, Adam was sitting in the car. He needed a break. He was looking at his phone, trying to get a little peace and quiet; he tried reading *The Economist*, whatever, but ended up on Quince's Instagram: a public profile, thousands of selfies, of course, pretty and annoying, the way he pouts his lips. A lazy gentleness in his eyes, that seems provocative, performative. And then there wasn't much else to do than put the phone in his other hand.

He went running afterwards, fast, he made the trip around the lake in good time. Angry and oxygenated at needing to relate to a light that was growing stronger. He tried to ignore Quince, but then Gry sent them out to pick elderflowers, and then she sent Quince in to play smart with the cooking, made him put face paint on him. She had no idea what she was doing.

Or did she?

It was like waking up. It made him want Gry more too, lifting her on top of him – she loved it.

And then Sejr went missing, and he fell to pieces. When they found Sejr, it was clear: life can change in an instant; life is precious, a brutal gift. Adam knows that he will take care of his family; he knows that he wants all he can get from life.

It had heightened his senses: how Quince occupied a space, a landscape, as the days passed. Emerging from the lake glittering wet, always half-undressed, clothes almost falling off him.

Adam gently bites Quince's lower lip.

Of course, there is the posturing, but Quince *is* different, a fantastic creature, a force. There's something about him that's hard to pin down, something familiar and foreign and raw. Quince, always talking and talking, but there's also something deeper to him, which he tries to distract you from. Actually, he's very distracting. Like the show with the hollandaise. Soaking himself in crayfish juice. Spilling peach juice down himself.

Adam smiles into the kiss.

Quince is other-worldly, unreal, or too real. It's like Quince has created an opening, in the forest, inside him, a parallel reality. Adam wants to have Quince like this.

He squeezes Quince's bicep. Quince stands straighter, looks at him, those honey eyes. Blinks. He's far away.

'What? What are you smiling at?'

Seriously, he sounds glazed. Adam feels it whistle through his spine, feeling himself getting hard.

'When you were sitting on the terrace, covered in peach juice.'

Quince glows.

'You noticed that?'

'You wanted me to notice that,' Adam says.

Quince looks down.

Adam almost can't control himself.

He wonders why it doesn't bother him.

He likes that he doesn't know what the next step is. They've gone off script.

Each touch feels new.

Like conquering something. Quince, of course, but also something inside himself.

He needs to.

*

Sylvia is tender with tiredness, the sorrow heavy in her body; her eyes are raw from crying, her chest, the redness drawn to her skin. It hurts, but it also feels honest, she tries to stay in it before she starts to articulate, narrate, how she feels. She's sitting in the kitchen, the light is grey and new, the night wants to be morning: this pure, early light reminds her of Karen; tasteful, austere.

Sylvia thinks that it's ridiculous, it's probably for the best that Danish weddings don't have that artful pause, that opportunity, like in American movies: Speak now or forever hold your peace. The chance to say something. The drama queen's moment. For what: a happy ending, an unhappy ending, an open ending?

She hears steps on the stairs, arms her nerves, presses the tears further down into her throat, locks them inside her chest.

Esben opens the door. He smiles. He waves without saying anything.

'I couldn't sleep,' he explains, and doesn't ask what she's doing, thank God.

She feels dizzy, but relieved that he's here, in the grey light. It must be a sign. For once, she doesn't think two or three times before acting.

*

Please, don't stop. Quince feels Adam's fingertips on his neck, gentler than he would have imagined; he feels Adam everywhere, his tongue, his warm hands, rough on his thin skin, his fingers searching for his hair, grasping his curls, as the kiss deepens. Adam grabs him harder, draws him into the kiss, and he gives in, and in, melts into it, sighing. Pulls back, runs his tongue along Adam's upper lip.

Quince feels Adam getting hard. He presses into him, glues his body to his, awestruck: Does he really want me? Adam laughs into his hair, and Quince feels himself getting too eager, but then Adam puts his hand on Quince's lower back, pulls him in, unabashed that Quince can feel his cock against his belly.

He's still an idiot.

Quince meets his eyes. Unzips Adam's jeans.

Quince kneels between the elderflowers, the creamy blossoms glowing in the dark, seventy full moons. And the blackbirds, his choir girls. He could swear that the nightingales are in the woods, and the blood rushes in his ears; a moment of adoration, eye contact, before he takes Adam's cock in his mouth, heavy and perfect. The taste of him. He moves his tongue slowly, savouring it, so that Adam feels him savouring it, doubts himself for a moment – maybe he should have played coy, played on the blushing – but oh well, now he's on his knees, tousled, hungry; a little late for that. He decides to be ravenous instead, take more in, he's sloppy, drooling; it's embarrassing, but it works, he feels Adam growing in his mouth, even harder – so it's like that – Quince moans, hums, lets himself be filled and disappears.

It builds up, the days fading behind them. Now, they're here. They can't stop. Quince realises the rhythm is up to him, so he goes slower, exaggeratedly slow, draws it out, delighted to finally have some control. Adam has been so difficult; he's vengeful enough to break contact, a clear spit thread trails from his lower lip to the head of Adam's cock; the evening air must be cold against the wet, thin skin warm with blood from beneath. Quince feels bad for the cold-sensitive skin for just a second, before Adam pushes himself deep into his mouth, an impatient tug on his hair that turns into a thumb resting on his neck; an apology, almost. And yet: We're done when I say we're done, and tears well up in Quince's eyes, a reflex, but also more. The sound of wetness: lips, tongues, spit, cock, and the blackbirds. He will draw this out as long as he can, Adam's hands in his hair, his voice hoarse, like something loosened.

*

Esben is sitting at the table, watching her. Sylvia feels the impression of his hand on her collarbone, where he pushed her away. Not hard, but not open to interpretation either. Her skin glows ashamedly. Sylvia reaches for his hand. He pulls it away, puts his face in his hands. They're both quiet.

He looks up at her.

'Do you know how messed up it is to say something like that to someone on the day of their wedding? That would be too much for anyone, and you know how I can get. You are just completely self-absorbed.'

Sylvia feels everything sinking inside her.

'I'm sorry. I was just thinking. That you should know. You were the one who said . . . that it would be lovely to live in a different way, if it were possible. Like Selma Lagerlöf.'

He takes a deep breath. It hurts how gently he says it.

'We're all suffering. We suffer, we yearn, everyone does. But it's shameless, what you're asking. You haven't thought it through. There's no coherence to it, it's just a crush, Syl, an escape. It's not anything that anyone besides yourself can do anything with. Even you can't do anything with it.'

Again, she imagines him in liturgical vestments, noble and impressive, even though she has no idea what he means.

'You think that you love me, but actually I'm just an object in your psychology. It's hurtful,' Esben says softly.

Sylvia feels like she's falling. The way that Esben

is able to take a step back, and ask: 'Is that the whole truth? No, of course not. Everything is more complicated and less enchanting than you think. You haven't even experienced real suffering yet.'

She lets it settle, a punishment, a lesson to be learned.

It feels like falling to her death. No, not a fatal fall. She thought she was Icarus, flying too close to the sun, hubristic, tragic, but epic. Now she feels like a moth idiotically bumping into a lamp.

Esben is placid again. His face is mild, gentle; he was upset with her, but not even for real. Is it really that simple? That he's getting married, that Karen makes him happy, that Sylvia should just let them be. Deep down she knows that this is precisely why she loves him: not because of his complexion, his intellect, but for his seriousness, his dignity, his sense of commitment (to his work, to Karen). Does she dream of being like that? It dawns on her: she respects him more than she respects herself.

'I just wanted you to know. In case you felt the same way.'

They're quiet. Esben looks at his hands.

'Okay. Let's say I tell Karen that I can't marry her. That I'm leaving her, so the two of us can be together. That would tear our group of friends apart, but let's say that we accept that. And then we'd have a life together, you and me. Just you and me. Is that what you want? Would you choose me? Is that the life you want?'

Is it? Her body feels awkward, cumbersome. She should be enraged, but she just feels heavy.

He stands and draws her into a hug, and she knows he's right, that it can't happen, that what she wants isn't inside him.

But what if it doesn't exist anywhere; what if it doesn't exist anywhere but inside of her?

She feels empty.

Lets go.

*

'Stop for a second. Get up.'

Quince stiffens. Reluctantly does as Adam says. They stand there in silence. What? Is he having second thoughts?

What kind of time is this for regret?

Adam fingers the button of Quince's shirt. As if he's running out the clock.

'I don't know . . .'

You've got to be kidding me.

Now he's got qualms?

Quince is about to storm off into the woods.

Adam looks at him, his hands hovering at the seam of Quince's jeans.

Oh. Quince grins, takes pity on him.

'Adam, you idiot! You can touch me. Everywhere. Even my cunt! *Please.*'

Adam pushes him up against the tree. Quince relishes it, Adam's bullishness. Twisting his shirt, the small, upholstered buttons and delicate fabric protesting.

'Just do it,' Quince says. 'Don't be afraid of being a cliché.' Adam tears open Quince's shirt, seeming like he's having fun. Pulls his own shirt over his head.

'These need to go too,' he says, and Quince opens his jeans, wriggles out of them. Quince is naked, and Adam lifts him, holding him up against the tree. It feels like a brag, but it also feels good. The bark is rough against his back. Quince throws his arms, his legs around Adam. He's weightless, trapped and free.

'Please . . .'

And then Adam is inside him, fucking him slowly, deeply. Quince is wet, he's totally gone. The bark is furrowed, etching small eager scratches into his back. He can live with that, reminds himself not to wear anything transparent to the wedding tomorrow; he can live with that too. He can deal with most things right now. He thinks: how is he here, how is this even happening, after all of these impossible days? Adam clutching him tight against the oak tree, a surrender. Inside him, in Adam.

I really didn't think he liked me.

Quince rests his head against the tree trunk, steals a glance at Adam, whose eyes are closed. He is attractive in an almost delicate way, blond hair clung in moist locks to his forehead, skin speckled red in strain, eagerness.

Was it even Adam that he wanted?

Of course. He looks like a god; he feels like one too.

But it was also a matter of enchantment, of bringing something to life, seeing if the spell worked.

He feels so good inside, he almost laughs.

He feels giddy with relief, triumph; a daybreak inside him. Quince has been so tense for so long, and now he feels sparks of light emanating from him, can barely control his movements, the small contractions, yelps, gasps. Thank goodness Adam is holding him tight. Is he slowing down? Can he tell that Quince is close? He groans.

'I have to put you down.'

Ha! He's tired. Quince glances at him, wipes some of the sweat off his forehead with the back of his hand: 'But you made *such* an effort.'

Adam snorts. Puts him down.

'Turn around.' Adam already has his hands on his hips, spins him to face the tree. A sound, when Adam sees the red scrapes. He touches them gently and it stings, but then Adam leans into him and he can feel Adam's chest, the broad warmth on his sore, screeching skin.

It feels just like it did in his fantasy. For a few deep breaths they stay like that, Adam just holding him. His arms feel strong; Quince can almost feel the swimming strokes in them, their steady strength. Quince lets himself be enveloped by them, rests his forehead against the trunk, and tears well in his eyes; he blinks. Not because the scratches hurt. Something is letting go, loosening in his chest.

A dark wave crashes over the euphoria, it hurts, but this is an even stronger feeling. He forces himself to stay in it, something deep inside him caves.

I want this. I want this tomorrow too, I think. I don't know if I can have it. But it feels new, incredible, to want it. Maybe I do want to be somebody's problem after all. Inside him, the moment protracts, pitches; just enjoy it while it lasts. He sniffs.

'Are you okay? Does it hurt? Was I too rough?'

Quince looks over his shoulder with a breathless grin, hoping that the tears make his eyes glitter, shameless, spent.

'No, it's so good. It's only good.'

Adam pauses, expectant.

Quince breathes deep into his belly.

'More, please,' he whispers.

'Can you handle it?' Adam asks.

Oh my God, Quince sighs, nodding, doesn't have a clever reply. Adam holds his body tight, a wall of warmth, contact, as he fucks him, harder. They must be steaming, Quince thinks, crashing against the bark, moaning in time with the thrusts, something building up in him. He can't speak coherently, whistles small sounds between clenched teeth. He squeezes his eyes shut and tries to control the ecstasy making his body collapse, rests his cheek on the tree, on Adam's arm, a bright universe unfolding behind his closed eyes.

He comes, coming undone with his mouth to

Adam's forearm, the woods dark green and humming around him, around them.

He gasps for air, tries to get the oxygen into his diaphragm, which is still trembling, the bark even rougher against his skin; he could collapse.

Then Adam turns him around, leans into Quince, pumps his hand a few times, his voice hoarse, hectic: 'Where?'

'Fuck, everywhere,' Quince gesticulates lazily, closes his eyes with a smile.

Adam folds on top of him, heavy, with a restrained noise. Quince feels the warm liquid on his upper body turning cold as it runs down him. Adam kneels in front of him, rests his face against his belly, catches his breath. Quince looks down at himself, his chest, his belly, bright red, the streak of semen.

Then Adam falls onto the grass, pulling Quince with him.

Their breathing is heavy and slow.

Here he is, lying in someone's arms.

It feels nice but also terrifying. What is happening, what happened, what was that dark wave, that earthquake inside him? Quince mumbles, talking to himself, foggy.

'You don't have to be so alone all the time . . .'

He feels Adam tense. Quince is about to clarify that he was talking to himself. But then Adam pulls him in tighter. Still not too tight. Quince tentatively throws a leg over Adam's body, then an arm, holds him, feels Adam relax. Did he hear a tremble in his breath?

The grass is fragrant beneath them. It's colder now. Adam fumbles for a piece of clothing with his free hand, and passes him his shirt. Something soft in Quince registers that Adam doesn't care that his clothes will get sticky. Though he is also a little irked: Typical cis men, thinking that because they can only come once that the show is over when they're tied, 1–1.

Quince puts a hand to Adam's cheek.

'We're done when I say we're done.'

*

Sylvia feels empty. Like the music is gone. The dreamy melodies and the ominous background chords that make her feel like she's acting in a musical about her own life, a transition to lighten the mood around the corner. But now she wonders if it was all in her head, if she was a fool. Everyone else is living in another film, with stricter demands of realism, a dogma film; or rather, the others are living in the real world, and it is bone dry, she acknowledges. She's the only one who has been fantasising about a midsummer utopia. Now she's ruined everything; now everything is quiet inside her. And the lake is quiet, coming to as the morning lightens.

She trudges down to the shore. The water isn't cold; the morning air is colder. She wades out, attempting to leave the smooth surface undisturbed; doesn't want to disturb anything ever again. She's tired of being impossible, of trying to connect with other people, forging through the forest, cracking off branches right and left. She walks through the reeds, into the gleam of the lobelia flowers shaking in the air. She feels the small buds on the ground, underfoot. She edges around them, carefully, she doesn't want to ruin anything else. She's tired. Tired of dreaming, of trying to be enchanting. Clearly, the world has no interest in reciprocating her efforts. She will never get over the humiliation, of having deluded herself into thinking it could work, having been so eager in her heart. Why can't she ever read the room and fit in, behave like a normal person? No one else is flipping out like her. They might dream of taking care of each other's kids, but they don't need to declare their love, force themselves on others. They sleep soundly through the night.

Now she's told the truth; you don't get any rewards for that. She has nothing left. What does she have that no one can take from her? A high tolerance for pain, a flair for drama, her yearning. She knows that she's composed of yearning, her principal element, and one moment with desire in her ascendant, the next with sadness.

She floats among the whitish blue, quavering flower stems; her nightgown is heavy, drawing her down, the water lapping quietly against her ear. It is comforting: the total indifference of the lake, the water slipping around her, as she lies there, floating in the reeds, bearing her heart; you can't keep making everyone else hold it for you, she thinks, but it's so heavy, and it's way too light, impetuous; it wants to go in every direction; it can't tell the difference between dreams and reality.

She doesn't have the energy.

Sylvia, our drama queen; would she really drown herself?

She shuts her eyes slightly. Turns to look into the camera, musters the irony not yet consumed by her humiliated grief.

'It will have to be without me as Ophelia . . . I'll just lie here licking my wounds. And eventually, I'll be ready to dream again, about the same thing or something else, to make the same old mistakes or new ones. Probably, I'll get back together with Charlie, but maybe I could be my own daddy first? And tomorrow, no, today I'll apologise and apologise, or maybe I'll be silent for once. But first, let me float in this water, rest among these flowers. As if I earned it.'

By the shore, she sees the fig tree she climbed up yesterday, when she was Sylvia Plath, dying of hunger, the figs calling out to her, falling to the ground. Something shifts inside her. Maybe that's enough? Maybe that would be enough for a whole life? Curling up in the nook of a tree, counting the figs, admiring their abundance.

'Maybe I'll take a stack of paper and write about every single fig; maybe I'll taste a few of them and pick some more and fall and hurt myself, crawl back up like a courageous idiot. Maybe I'll be fickle. Maybe I'll fall in love with everything. Be engaged to everything. I don't need to get married. What do I want to do with the rest of my life? Maybe, I will just sit in a tree, dreaming and writing. And so what if nothing ever happens.'

And because she's lying there, living on, she sees two figures emerge from the forest and can't believe her eyes. She watches one of them draw the other in, a long embrace at the edge of the woods, maybe a whisper, before they return inside. Everything lifts inside her, quiet as air, and a few salty drops mingle with the lake's fresh water.

Miracles can happen.

That is enough.

It doesn't have to be her own.

Day 7

The light grows.

Karen wakes up. She feels rested; she's slept soundly through the night. She needs to get up and get going, take a shower; onwards and upwards; soon she'll be back to reality. But first: the wedding. It'll be easy, getting married is no big deal.

Acknowledgements

A debt of gratitude

Because I'm so awfully good at seeking help and attention, I have many to thank. What a great privilege: to be beholden.

I want to thank the generous people in my life who have read along and discussed the book with me while it was being written. Thank you for being wiser than me and for all of your time and encouragement, for telling me off, for drinks and memes and inspiration, for clever remarks and unchecked chemistry, for being irresistible and quotable. For being friends, colleagues, inconvenient objects of desire and for being ready to talk about how volatile and magical those categories can be.

Thank you to Jeppe for the title (and for being a catty queen trapped in a straight man's body). To Ane Kirstine, Selma, Johannes, Elin, Anne, Cecilie, Caroline, Storm, Liv, Lucia, Johanne, Tatiana, Mia, Cecilie, Lasse, Kathrine, Nanna, Sophie-Lønne, Felix, Gyrith, Nina and many others for readings, hype and loaning me your confidence. Thank you to *Weekendavisen* for having an admirably nonchalant leave policy. To my editor, Iben – how wonderful, that someone could be such a careful and staunch reader. I am also happily indebted to all of the jesters of the internet, for jokes, tweets, tumblrisms that I have borrowed as punchlines.

I'm so grateful that I didn't write this book in solitude, and I owe you all.

Thank goodness – there isn't any shame in debt, or in a debt of gratitude. There's a modern obsession with being debt-free. As a wise writer once said, when I had the chance to interview her: 'It's a good thing that we are indebted to one another, that we are bound together. It's good to owe each other something.'

We don't need to be so alone all the time.

Hell isn't other people. Hell is logistics; and you can work with those.

A special thanks to Amanda Herskind Ernst. For the love. And for everything.

I love you.